THE GODCHILD

Other books by Stephen Alter

NEGLECTED LIVES
SILK AND STEEL

The Godchild

Stephen Alter

ANDRE DEUTSCH

For Hilary Rubinstein

First published 1987
by André Deutsch Limited
105–106 Great Russell Street London WC1B 3LJ

Phototypeset in Sabon by
David John Services Ltd
Maidenhead, Berks

Printed in Great Britain by
WBC Bristol

British Library Cataloguing in Publication Data

Alter, Stephen
  The godchild.
  I. Title
  813'.54[F]   PS3551.L77

ISBN 0–233–97963–8

CONTENTS

PART ONE

THE GODCHILD

1

PART TWO

BURNT OFFERINGS

7

PART THREE

THE COMPOUND

67

PART FOUR

MAMTA

103

PART FIVE

DEPARTURE

159

I KNEW that Mamta would never become a Christian. She was so different from the rest of us. Even when she spoke about being baptized and asked us to tell her stories from the Bible, I knew that there was something in her nature which kept Mamta apart from us, a knowledge of darker secrets, perhaps, a kind of mystery. Or maybe it was my own desire to keep her the way she was which made me feel like this, a need to separate her from ourselves. I did not want her to become like us. I loved the way she spoke, with her tribal dialect. I loved the way she braided flowers in her hair. I loved the way she moved, the way her eyes shone, the sound of her singing as she rocked her daughter to sleep. Mamta was unlike anyone I had ever known.

I realized that she was different from the first day I saw her but I did not understand what it was that I had sensed in Mamta until one day she took me to a country fair. The fair was held each year in Pipra but I had never gone before. My parents didn't like the idea but I pestered them so much, they finally let me go. I was twelve and Mamta was about sixteen. We set off together from the compound, just as it was getting dark and took a shortcut from behind the hospital and crossed the fields near the cold storage plant and the firing range. We walked some distance and came to a crossroads, with a few mud huts and a temple standing on a low hill. The fairground was on the other side of the hill. I had seen it once before, just an open field of hard-packed clay and an enormous gateway with plaster elephants and rampant tigers painted black and yellow. It looked as though someone had started to build a palace long ago and suddenly changed their mind.

There was a village road coming in from the hills and it was lined with bullock carts. Villagers were walking along in groups, going to or returning from the fair. Children were clutching toy bugles, whistles of brittle plastic and limp balloons. They were dressed in their brightest clothes and the women were adorned with jewelry.

As we came in sight of the fairground, I was amazed by the circle of tents which filled the open field, the striped canopies and banners. The gateway was freshly painted in different colours and festooned with flowers and streamers. Two loudspeakers were strung up on either side, blaring out a cinema tune. The static shredded the singer's voice, which sounded almost inhuman. Behind the clamour and noise was the rhythmic chugging of a diesel generator. Even from a distance, I could feel a rush of excitement as if the air was charged with electricity.

We joined the crowd of villagers who were going to the fair. Near the entrance there were rows of stalls selling sweets and white, crumbly pastries. There were images made of sugar, Hindu gods and goddesses. Swarms of bees hovered over the confectionary. A man with a trained bear came by, leading the shaggy animal on a chain. He tapped his stick against the bear's snout and made it stand up and fold its paws. On every side there were hawkers selling cheap trinkets, plastic buttons and nylon ribbons. Their shouts and voices clashed with each other like a good humoured argument. I stayed close to Mamta, a little afraid of all the noise and confusion.

We stopped to watch a juggler, who balanced knives above his head, their silver blades pointing down. Most of the people at the fair were tribals like Mamta. They wore bright colours, the women with flowered scarves over their heads and full skirts, decorated with bright prints and mirror-work embroidery. Their arms were covered with bracelets of metal, ivory and glass. Their eyes were blackened with kajal. Each village group seemed to have its own distinctive colour, some in matching green, others in red. Their faces were full of laughter and gaiety. The men and women moved in segregated groups and the children scampered about barefoot, their legs covered with dust, caught up in their frenzied games. The tube lights added to the air of excitement, while the scratchy music and the sound of the generator set a throbbing tempo.

At one end of the fairground were the entertainments, the ferris wheels and carousels, along with several small circuses and sideshows. We wandered slowly towards the giant wheel turning

2

overhead. It was decorated with coloured bulbs and there were four men inside who climbed the struts to make it go around.

I noticed a large sign near one of the tents. There was a frightening looking beast painted on canvas, a demonic creature with two heads and vicious looking fangs. It had a shaggy body like a bear and a long forked tail.

"What's that?" said Mamta, pointing to the sign.

"Some sort of circus," I said. "There's supposed to be a two-headed monster inside."

"Really?" said Mamta.

"I'm sure it's fake," I said, trying to act uninterested even though I was scared of what it might really be. "It's probably just an old hyena," I said, "or some monkey with dyed fur or something."

Just then, a shrill cry came out of the loudspeaker above the tent. It was a strange, artificial sort of cackle.

Mamta looked at me and laughed.

"Let's have a look," she said.

"It really won't be much," I said, making a face. "A waste of money."

"How much does it cost?" said Mamta.

"Eight annas," I said, looking at the sign again. I was frightened. I didn't want to see this monster.

But Mamta had already gone to the entrance of the tent and taking money from the purse which she kept in the waistband of her skirt, she paid for both of us. The proprietor was a withered old man, with a single buck tooth which jutted out over his lower lip and an enormous magenta turban. He wore a gold earring and on his fingers there were several rings of different sizes with multi-coloured stones. He waved us inside with a surly gesture of his hand. A pair of villagers came out. They looked at Mamta with alarm.

Inside the flap of the tent, there was a stuffed crocodile suspended on a wire and coming apart at the seams. An old woman was squatting in one corner of the tent. She got up stiffly and greeted us. I guessed that she was the wife of the man outside. The woman was wearing ivory bracelets all the way above her elbows. These rattled when she moved. The tent was crammed full of an odd assortment of objects. There was the skeleton of an animal about the size of a dog and two trophy heads of deer looking forlornly down from the bamboo poles of the tent. On one of the tables were more than a dozen bottles which contained a variety of snakes coiled up in alcohol. There was a smell inside the tent which reminded me of the laboratory at the hospital.

The old woman beckoned as she went to the far end of the tent and pulled aside a tattered curtain. There stood a wooden case with little doors painted green and yellow. I watched the woman as she fumbled at the latch and opened the case with shaking hands.

The monster lay inside the case, arranged on a narrow shelf with two light bulbs on either side. It was imprisoned in a heavy glass jar and like the snakes, preserved in alcohol. There was no forked tail or shaggy coat as advertized on the board outside. Instead the skin was wrinkled and colourless, almost translucent. There were two heads, four arms and four legs.

Mamta made a low, choking sound in her throat. I glanced at her and saw the look on her face, an expression of emptiness and awe. The hideous specimen in the bottle seemed almost alive. There were several coins on the shelf beside the bottle, which someone had placed there as an offering. I pulled at Mamta's arm, trying to take her away, but she resisted. The smell of the tent enveloped us and I felt light-headed.

Mamta folded her hands and lowered her head. She said nothing and her eyes were closed. As I watched, she knelt down before the creature and then lay flat on the ground, her face in the dirt. I was terrified and didn't know what to do, whether I should run out of the tent and escape, leaving Mamta prostrate before the beast.

But then, something came over me. I looked at the beast once again and it appeared to be talking to itself, one set of lips close to the ear of the second head, a silent conversation with a hint of guilt, two separate faces on a single torso, arms and legs entwined. Their whispering seemed to be a confession as if they were ashamed of their nakedness. The beast no longer seemed obscene. The faces were not ugly, but strangely beautiful, with hair like corn silk and pale grey eyes, a freakish beauty, the divided parts of their bodies combined into a flawed yet perfect human child, their hands and arms, their buttocks, each completely formed. There was a single cord which had tied them to their mother, the one inseverable artery which had sustained them in the womb. I no longer felt revulsion or nausea, no pity or sadness. It was not a beast but entirely human, not dead but immortal. I felt a sense of wonder and was unafraid. Its presence filled the tent like a vision and I imagined

4

the two small bodies merging into one, becoming a single person.

At last Mamta raised herself from the ground and taking some coins from her purse, she placed them on the shelf beside the bottle. The old woman shut the case, her ivory bracelets rattling like bones. Mamta took me by the hand and led me out of the tent. The blaring music and the crowds engulfed us once again, the chaos of the fair. I was crying now, the tears running down my face. I was confused, not sure if I had seen something wonderful or if I had committed a terrible sin. Then Mamta looked at me and laughed. She was herself again.

"Were you frightened, Gideon?" she asked.

"A little bit," I said.

Mamta squeezed my hand and I pressed my face against her shoulder, to wipe the tears away. People stared at us but their eyes seemed to dissolve into the shadows. My legs were giving way. I was flooded with a feeling of gladness. I felt as if I had been cleansed and my tears were those of absolution. It was as if the sight of the child in the bottle, its grotesque presence had brought me closer to Mamta's world, her fears, her anguish. The creature in the bottle was not a beast or a demon but a child of God.

After some time, Mamta and I got onto the ferris wheel and rode it round and round until the whole world was spinning beneath us.

Part Two

BURNT OFFERINGS

ONE

TRICIA SAT next to the window, staring out. She was a slender girl, her hair bobbed short and brushed behind her ears, which made her look like a tomboy. There was an alert, almost fearful expression in her eyes. Her hands were clasped together, as if to keep them still. An old woman sat on the far end of the seat watching Tricia with matriarchal disdain, feet tucked beneath her haunches, jowls quivering as she chewed her paan. The moving air was fresh, though warm. The train had been passing through jungle for some time now, miles of scrubby acacia trees with twisted branches, patches of broad-leafed forest and bamboo, sprayed with sunlight. The cadence of the wheels seemed to dull Tricia's senses, as though it were an echo – the cruising drone of the jetliner, the humming of the air-conditioner in the hotel room at Delhi – a monotonous sound, which slipped out of hearing, so that she was unconscious of it, suspended in silence.

Their compartment was a first class coupé, two berths against one wall, a mirror, luggage rack and table. A fine layer of soot and dust covered everything. Overhead were two fans in wire cages, whirring softly. Next to the mirror there was a chain with a wooden handle painted red and beneath it the stencilled lettering:

FOR EMERGENCY ONLY – Pull to Stop Train.

Fine of Rs.2,000 or three months imprisonment for misuse.

The night before, when Tricia had boarded the train at Delhi station, she found the compartment crowded with a family of ten,

7

the old woman seated in their midst. Thinking that she had made a mistake, Tricia checked with the conductor, but after inspecting her ticket and consulting his charts, he pointed to the upper berth. The coolies stowed her suitcases inside, while Tricia wondered how they were all going to travel in the same compartment together. One of the men stood up politely and made room for Tricia on the seat, but the rest of the family eyed her with distrust. When the whistle blew, one by one they each touched the old woman's feet and kissed her cheeks goodbye. The train was already moving when the last of them made his obeisance and hurried out the door. The old woman gave an asthmatic sigh, as if exhausted by the farewell and the obsequious devotion of her children. She spoke to Tricia in Hindustani, her voice gruff with phlegm. Tricia shook her head helplessly, not understanding.

There was a disturbing hint of madness in the old woman's eyes, opaque with cataracts. She wore a pair of spectacles and the thick lenses seemed to magnify her blindness. Once again the old woman spoke in Hindustani, this time a question. Tricia shrugged her shoulders.

"I'm afraid I don't know what you're saying."

The grandmother looked puzzled and pointed a finger – her nails were pink – asking, "Indian?"

"No, actually, I'm an American," Tricia replied, but the woman knew no English. She was also deaf and put a hand to her ear.

"USA! United States!" Tricia had to shout, as if she were a cheerleader.

"Mother India? Father?" asked the old woman in broken English.

Tricia smiled again and shook her head. There was no way to explain, no pantomime or sign language she could use to make herself understood.

The old woman finally got bored with the interrogation and reached for a cloth bag on the seat beside her. Fumbling, she produced an aluminium box and opened it. Tricia watched her choose a heart-shaped leaf, which she placed flat on the lid of the box. Her gnarled fingers moved deftly as she smeared a red paste on the leaf. The box contained a number of sachets and bottles from which the old woman sprinkled different powders. Using a strange instrument, which looked something like a pair of miniature shears, she cut a betel nut into slivers, then added a pinch of

8

tobacco. She hesitated before putting a green cardamom in the centre of the leaf, folded the whole thing into a bite-sized morsel and popped it into her mouth. She chewed the paan contentedly, while Tricia made her bed on the upper berth.

After a while, Tricia noticed that the old woman's cheeks were bulging with juice. Having no spitoon, she glanced around the compartment, then casually spat a gout of red saliva on the floor. Tricia watched with surprise and disgust as the woman wiped her mouth on the corner of her sari.

"Why don't you spit out the window?" said Tricia, pointing.

The old woman said nothing, her eyes glazed with satisfaction. She spat once again, as though suffering from some kind of internal hemorrhage.

"Not on the floor!" said Tricia, "Please!"

But the old woman paid no attention. A piece of betel nut was stuck in her teeth. Her face twisted into a grimace, as she tried to work it free with her tongue. When that did not succeed, she poked about with her fingers and finally removed her dentures altogether. They were stained a gruesome red and she put them down carefully on top of the aluminium box. The sight of the discoloured teeth made Tricia turn her face away. The old woman puckered her hollow cheeks and smacked her gums. Then with meticulous care, she cleaned the palate of her dentures, using a handkerchief, before replacing them in her mouth.

Almost immediately, she began to make herself another paan. For a long time Tricia just watched, with a growing sense of revulsion. She felt threatened by the old woman. There was something obscene about her withered features, the painted nails, her red-stained lips and orange tongue. The train shook and rattled as it gathered speed, the last lights of Delhi flashing by in the darkness. Tricia wondered where the old woman was going, but did not ask. Probably to visit other children and grandchildren, she thought, imagining them standing dutifully on some distant platform, waiting for the old woman to arrive, so that they could garland her and touch her feet, so they could worship her.

Tricia took off her sandals and climbed up into bed. Since leaving New York, she had passed through two sleepless nights and a day, foreshortened into the space of thirty hours, after which everything took on the quality of a dream, a hallucination.

As she lay on the berth, Tricia's mind and nerves seemed to be racing with the train. She could hear laughter coming from the compartment next door and someone was playing a transistor radio. Despite the fans, the air was hot and Tricia was scared of rolling off her berth. Sometime after midnight she finally fell asleep, listening to the distant retching of the engine as it sped through the night. Tricia dreamed that she had found her mother, a thin, crippled woman sitting on the floor of an empty room. But when she tried to embrace her mother the woman shrieked at her in a strange language and showed no sign of recognition.

When Tricia opened her eyes, she was aware that the train had stopped. The blue night-light was on overhead but there was daylight coming through the slatted window. She could hear shouts and yells of people getting off and on the train. Thinking she had overslept, Tricia got down in a panic. The old woman was awake.

"Is this Pipra?" asked Tricia.

The old woman just stared, not comprehending.

Tricia unlatched the door and slid it open, hurrying barefoot down the corridor. The conductor was standing near the toilets talking to another man.

"Pipra?" she asked, afraid the train was going to start.

The conductor shook his head with boredom and held up two fingers.

"After two stations," he said, in English, without removing the cigarette from his mouth. He and the other man were staring at the front of her shirt, which had come unbuttoned.

Tricia turned away quickly and went back into the compartment, where the old woman sat with the impassive repose of an evil deity. The paan stains on the floor looked like blood, as though she had performed a sacrifice during the night. Tricia opened the window to get some fresh air into the compartment. The early morning light was a blue-grey colour. It was only five o'clock. Tricia thought of going back to bed but she was wide awake.

On the platform, just outside the window of the compartment, was a cement bench. A family with two young children had converted it into a temporary home. Their belongings, which consisted of a large bundle of rags, a tin canister, an axe and two blackened pots, were neatly arranged on one end of the bench. The younger child was lying on a piece of patchwork cloth. The other child, a boy, was standing with his back to Tricia playing with something in his hands.

They looked to her like gypsies – though Tricia had never seen a gypsy in her life. There was something mediæval about them. The woman was dressed in a faded black skirt with red and yellow embroidery along the. hem. She wore a tight-fitting blouse of the same colours. Her arms were adorned with ivory bracelets. Covering her head and shoulders was an orange scarf which she had tucked into the waist of her skirt. Her face was partly hidden by the scarf but Tricia could see that she wore a silver necklace and rings in her ears and nose. The baby was naked and the boy was wearing a frayed pair of shorts. He had an amulet around his neck. They seemed to have spent the night on the platform.

Tricia slid her suitcase out from under the seat, to get her camera. There was a simplicity about the scene which attracted her. She wanted a picture of the woman and her children. The mother had a plain and brooding face. She spoke to the boy in a whisper. Tricia caught her eye, but she looked away. The light was poor and Tricia adjusted the aperture, focussing on the silver necklace. When the camera clicked, it was a very slight sound but the woman heard it. Instantly she turned to face Tricia with an expression between fear and anger. Tricia put the camera away, feeling as though she had intruded.

A few minutes later, the woman's husband arrived from the direction of the station. He was a thin, tubercular figure with an enormous moustache twisted up at the ends. He wore a loose turban of red, a torn shirt and striped pyjamas. There was something forbidding about him. His face was mottled with smallpox. He squatted down and took a cigarette out of his pocket. Lighting it, he was careful not to singe his moustache, holding his head back from the flame. The woman said something to him and he turned and glanced at Tricia, squinting his eyes with distrust. Then he spoke to the boy who was teasing the baby with a feather. The boy shook his head and did not reply. His father raised his voice and made a threatening gesture with his hand. Reluctantly the boy came across the platform to Tricia's window. He put on a pitiful expression, as though complaining against his father, and lifted both hands, begging for money.

Tricia felt angry with the father, who sat there watching with a bored expression, the smoke from his cigarette filtering through his moustache. Tricia shook her head at the boy, refusing to give him anything. The child was pleading loudly, repeating the same word over and over again, "Bhooka! Bhooka! Bhooka!" He had long reddish hair and his navel protruded from his belly. There were scabs on his knees. When Tricia continued to refuse, he grabbed onto the bars of the window and clambered up to see inside. His tone had changed, less pathetic now, almost as though he were teasing her. He craned his neck to see the old woman.

The baby on the bench began to cry and the mother took it down. She slipped a breast from beneath her blouse and put the child to the nipple. The old woman shouted at the boy, who was crouched on the edge of the window like a monkey. He made a face at her, leering through the bars. The whistle blew and the carriages creaked and began to slide forward. The boy continued to beg, reaching his hand through the window. Tricia resisted stubbornly, but as the train began to pick up speed she grew afraid. The boy kept hanging on as they went past the station. "Bhooka! Bhooka!" Tricia shook her head and bit her lip. The boy looked ahead over his shoulder, his hair blowing across his eyes. He grinned at Tricia as though daring her not to give him money. She wanted to tell him to get down, to push him off. The train was moving much faster now and Tricia desperately tried to find a coin in her pocket to give him, but before she could, the boy jumped free of the carriage and they left the platform behind.

TWO

THE BHISHTI filled his goatskin water-bag at the pump and began laying the dust near the out-patients' clinic, a jet of water spraying from between his fingers. He dug his elbow into the taut skin of the mushuq to maintain the pressure. Pellets of water fell in an arc on the dry ground and the musky odour of wet earth was tempered with the smell of disinfectant. The bhishti worked his way slowly forward, hunched over the weight of his mushuq, marking out an area of sterility.

The mission hospital at Pipra was a single-story brick building, encircled by verandahs. Two neem trees stood in front, their branches forming a canopy of leaves over the entrance and casting cool shadows on the ground. The motor road from the town passed in front of the hospital and continued west. There was no sign, only a painted cross on one of the pillars of the gate. Several cycle rickshaws were parked outside, waiting for a fare back to town. A vendor had arranged his display case on the parapet wall over the culvert, selling cigarettes and matches to the villagers squatting in clusters under the neem trees, families and friends of patients. Across the road was the mission compound, with the yellow church and decrepit bungalows, surrounded by a low brick wall and a hedge of thorns. The compound was lifeless compared to the hospital, which hummed with the incessant murmur of voices, as people waited for something to happen, a recovery, a relapse, a death. It was still early in the morning, seven o'clock, and yet there was already a crowd at the hospital.

Part of the verandah had been converted into an open air ward, to make room for the more infectious patients inside. A man lay in traction, his plaster leg suspended from the ceiling and weighted with a couple of bricks. A boy with his neck in a brace sat on a cot, while his mother poured water into his mouth. Three malarial patients squatted in a row at the edge of the verandah, wrapped in blankets despite the heat. They watched the bhishti as he approached the trees, his mushuq much lighter now. The villagers moved aside as he sprinkled the ground where they had been sitting, the powdery dust turning a reddish colour. The air was stagnant, humid. A flock of parakeets alighted on the neem trees for a moment and then flew on with angry screams.

From the workshop at the rear of the hospital came the sound of hammering. Several of the villagers wandered towards the noise, curious. A small group had already gathered at the workshop, which was nothing but an open shed with a corrugated tin roof. Dr Fry stood in the centre, wearing a stained canvas apron, his hands and arms covered with grease to the elbows. The banging had ceased and the crowd stood silent, watching Fry, the sunburnt face and rumpled white hair. He was a tall, sturdy man, with a smear of grease on the side of his nose, where he had wiped the perspiration away. Oblivious of the crowd, he watched Gyani tighten the last bolts.

A genuine 'Rube Goldberg', he thought. We'll just have to keep our fingers crossed. The mechanism is okay, it's just so hard to get the darned thing to hold air. His lower back gave a jolt of pain. He had strained it earlier in the morning. They had been working all night. Dr Fry reached behind to massage the base of his spine and left a black handprint on the seat of his khaki shorts. Maybe I should have put a governor on the shaft. Not enough time, as usual.

The crowd was full of speculation, guessing among themselves the purpose of this machine. They could see that it was a barrel attached to the front end of a bicycle. One of the boys from town suggested that it might be a generator. Another, more knowledge-able, said it had something to do with Mor Singh's daughter, who had been sick for almost a week. As Dr Fry walked around to the other side, the crowd moved back to give him room.

The barrel was one of six which had carried his sea freight after the last furlough. It still had his name and address painted on the side: Dr Eugene Fry, Mission Hospital, Pipra, Dist. Madinpur, INDIA. He had removed the lid and welded a conical attachment over the mouth of the barrel, a kind of metal apron with a hole at the end. This opened as a hatch. The barrel was lined with a rubber sleeve, the tube from a tractor tyre which had been cut to size and glued in place. The barrel lay on its side, attached to a bed-frame by four metal brackets. Its base had been punctured at two places, admitting a pair of hose pipes. These were held in position and sealed with rubber gaskets. The hose pipes were attached to an old army-surplus foot-pump, which Fry had dug out of his store room. He'd bought it in the States ten years ago, at the same time as he bought the rubber dinghy, one of those useless purchases. He'd had a plan to float down the canal, but somehow never got around to it. The pump was as good as new, once he cleaned it up. You can never tell what's going to come in handy, he thought. Maybe some day I'll find a use for the dinghy as well.

The trick had been to reverse the pump so that it sucked air out of the barrel and created a vacuum. For a while he'd almost given up, thinking it wouldn't work. But in the end, after fiddling with the valve for several hours, he had succeeded. The rest was simple mechanics, an elementary cam-shaft attached to a rocker arm which operated the pump. He'd added a flywheel to help regulate the speed. All of this was housed in a wooden box at the foot of the barrel. Then he'd rigged up a bamboo scaffolding at the end of the bed and after taking his bicycle apart, removing the wheels, brakes and mudguards, he fitted what was left onto the bamboo frame and fixed the rear sprocket to the end of the shaft which protruded from the box. By now, some of the people watching had decided that it was a rickshaw. Or maybe a newfangled meat grinder, Fry thought, amused by their curiosity. No one had dared to ask him for an explanation. The whole thing had taken a day and a half to construct. The parts which had to be turned on a lathe and welded were done at a workshop downtown.

"All right, let's get her inside," he said.

Six men lifted the machine on their shoulders and carried it into the hospital, through one of the back doors. Dr Fry crossed over to the pump where the bhishti was refilling his mushuq. Using detergent, Fry scrubbed up a lather on his hands and forearms. It took more than one washing to remove the grease and even after he'd finished there were stains in his calluses and around the edges of his fingernails. Bending down at the pump sent a current of pain through his body, agony. He moaned as he straightened up and considered taking a muscle relaxant.

Dr Fry went inside and beckoned to a young nurse, Sister Rita, a plain girl, her eyes large but unaligned. She was dark-skinned and wore white stockings beneath her starched uniform, which made her look as though she were an albino from the waist down.

"Yes, doctor," she said.

"I'll need an ironing board and a plastic sheet, plenty of pillows."

"Yes, doctor."

As though to prove his point, as though he needed a reason for building the contraption which now stood at the far end of the ward, looking like an exercycle attached to a cement mixer, the electricity went off. The fans which had been churning the air died all at once, slowing down and finally coming to a halt. The humidity seemed to close in around him and Fry could feel his shirt sticking to his shoulder blades.

In the bed next to the machine lay a young girl, ten or twelve, but small for her age. He had measured her, three feet nine inches. Three feet exactly from her toes to her shoulders. Sister Tara stood beside the bed and from time to time she would massage the girl's chest. The girl was fighting for each breath, hardly able to get the air into her lungs. There was a cylinder of oxygen next to the bed.

Yesterday he'd done a tracheotomy. Dr Fry leaned over to check the tube in her throat and a rivulet of sweat ran down his face. He stepped back and mopped his forehead with a hankerchief. There was now a dull ache in his back, relentless, much worse than the sudden jolts of pain. Still September, he thought, another month and a half of hot weather, the worst time of year, with the fever and epidemics, the air so heavy that you wonder if the sky hasn't fallen on top of you, the dead-weight of the atmosphere. He brushed a fly off the girl's hair.

Sister Rita arrived with the ironing board. Fry removed the legs and slipped it inside the barrel. Too long by a couple of inches. Gyani was sent to fetch a saw and as they all waited, Fry put a couple of pillows inside and fussed with the rubber sleeve. The girl's parents watched in silence. They were farmers from a nearby village, the father in roughspun cotton, his wife much younger, her face shrouded in the pulloo of her sari.

Gyani began to saw the end of the board, bracing it on the edge of the bed-frame with his knee, the sawdust falling in a fine yellow trail on the brick floor. Nothing as satisfying as a sharp saw, thought Fry, though the sound of it and the sight of the steel teeth ripping through the wood reminded him of the tearing sensation in his back, as though the muscles and tendons had been shredded.

The ironing board now fitted nicely. He put extra pillows on either side and covered it all with first a plastic and then a cotton sheet, tucking them in carefully. He did not let himself be hurried. Sister Tara helped him lift the girl inside, feet first. She was emaciated, with tangled black hair, her eyes closed. The other patients in the ward sat up to see what was happening and the screen windows were darkened by the faces of people watching from the verandah. Dr Fry took no notice of his audience. He was too absorbed in his work, making sure that the girl's head was properly supported. After checking to see if the rubber sleeve fitted comfortably around her neck, he closed the hatch. For a brief moment, he thought how she looked like one of those women magicians saw in half.

His back was hurting too much to risk climbing onto the bicycle, so he gestured to one of the girl's relatives, a young man of sixteen, who got willingly onto the seat. Dr Fry spoke softly.

"Now don't pedal too fast and stop if I tell you."

The boy nodded and began to cycle. The sprockets turned and from inside the box came the chugging of the pump as it started to suck out air from the barrel. The end of the rubber sleeve drew tight against the girl's skin. She whimpered and moved her head. As the pressure dropped inside the barrel, a valve opened with a sigh, the intake of air. Everyone in the ward jumped at the sound, except Fry, who had been waiting for it. He smiled as the pump continued steadily. The girl lay still and after several minutes it was obvious that she was breathing more easily now. Dr Fry checked her pulse and listened carefully, signalling to the boy to pedal faster. The rhythm of the pump and the sound of the valve quickened. More than a hundred eyes were watching the machine intently. Dr Fry opened the box at the foot of the barrel and looked inside. When he spoke again, it was to the girl's father, but he said it loud enough for all to hear.

"As soon as the boy gets tired, someone else can take his place. Everybody can have a try, but not too fast, just keep her breathing easily. There are enough people around her doing nothing. They might as well get a little exercise." He pointed to the windows which were still darkened by the faces peering in.

"Will this machine cure her?" asked the father.

"No, it will only help her to breath, that's all."

Seeing the farmer's uncertainty, he tried to explain.

"This is an iron lung." He said it first in English and then in Hindustani, but realized that the literal translation made no sense. He put his hands on the man's chest and back, pressing to show him how it worked. This revealed the purpose to those who were watching from the windows and they began to explain to each other, in an eager commotion of voices.

But there's no way to explain polio, is there, he thought, catching himself off-guard. The hours without sleep closed in upon him and he could not fight the sadness. He turned away from the girl, knowing that he had done all that he could and yet with a sense of impotence and frustration. Prayer, he thought, but at that moment there was no conviction left in him, only the emptiness of a yawn, the rawness in his eyes and the persistent nagging of his back. Leaving Sister Tara in charge, he went outside. His watch read eight o'clock. He hurried to the gate, tucking in his shirt tails and quickly got into a rickshaw.

"Railway station," said Dr Fry.

THREE

"CHRISTIAN?" asked the old woman.

"Stop pointing at me," said Tricia, sharply.

Again the woman spat and Tricia turned away, tasting a sour bitterness at the back of her throat.

She could see the hills now, like purple shadows against the sky. They were much higher than she'd expected, rising up out of the forest in jagged profile. The train was travelling parallel to the hills, through open jungle, with scattered scrub and acacia trees. Tricia felt as though she had seen the hills before, maybe in a dream.

The forest was still green from the late monsoon, but there was a veil of dust in the air. A little further on were fields, ploughed but unplanted. The clods of earth were a grey, infertile colour. There were several mud huts with cattle tethered outside. The train slowed down as it crossed a bridge over a shallow canal. They entered the periphery of the town, scattered cement houses gradually getting closer together until they fitted against each other, with narrow alleys in between. They passed a line of abandoned freight cars. PIPRA – the bold lettering, black on yellow jumped out at Tricia from the wall of a water tower. Here I am, thought Tricia, feeling apprehension and excitement at the same time. It was as though the name of the town itself became, all at once, more than just a word. Pipra had always been a place which Tricia had never quite believed in, never accepted as anything more than an imaginary town. But now it became real, no longer far away or make believe.

The carriage glided to a stop alongside the platform and shouting voices seemed to converge around her. Two coolies in faded pink shirts and turbans, with brass badges on their arms threw open the door of the compartment. Tricia pointed to her suitcases and followed them into the corridor, without looking back at the old woman.

As she stepped down onto the platform, Tricia didn't know where to turn. There was confusion at the station, though it seemed as if she was the only person getting off the train. The coolies were jabbering at her, assuming that she spoke Hindustani. Tricia held up a hand, trying to silence them. A beggar shuffled forward, holding up a leperous paw and moaning pathetically. Tricia took the coins from her pocket and dropped them in his bowl, more to get him to go away than from any immediate feeling of charity.

At the same moment, she caught sight of Dr Fry. Tricia knew that it had to be him, even though he was a much larger man than she had imagined. He came hurrying through the gate, peering over the heads of the crowd. Tricia pushed her way towards him.

"Hello," she said, putting out her hand. "Dr Fry?"

"Are you Patricia?" he said.

They greeted each other with self-conscious formality. His hand did not feel at all like a doctor's hand, she thought. It was rough and calloused.

"I don't think I would have recognized you," he said.

"I didn't know whether you'd even remember who I was," said Tricia, unable to keep from staring at him. He spoke softly, with an indistinct American accent. Fry grinned as he studied her with his watery blue eyes. His face was unshaven and he was slightly stooped.

He couldn't stop smiling at her. She looked so young to him, still a girl, though he had figured out her age to twenty-one.

"Where's your luggage?" he asked.

Tricia pointed to the coolies who stood patiently with the suitcases on their heads. Dr Fry beckoned to them and took her by the arm. At the gate, there was a crush of passengers hurrying to get on the train before it left for other destinations. So many bodies packed into the station made the air suffocating. Outside, the sun was harsh, merciless. More than a dozen cycle rickshaws ringing their bells, several horse-driven tongas and one or two dilapidated taxis stood in the open yard. Tricia watched as the coolies loaded her luggage onto a rickshaw.

"Are we going to ride in that?" she asked, looking worried.

Dr Fry gave her a reassuring smile.

"Don't worry, it's perfectly safe," he said.

He paid the coolies before Tricia could find her money and then helped her climb into the rickshaw. It made her think of a giant tricycle. They had to straddle the suitcases. Dr Fry took his place beside her on the narrow seat and gave a word of encouragement to the rickshaw man. As Fry shifted his weight, Tricia noticed that he winced with pain.

20

"Are you comfortable?" she asked.

"Fine thanks," he said. "I wrenched my back this morning. Getting old, that's all."

"You shouldn't have bothered to come and meet me," she said, noticing that he looked exhausted.

Dr Fry winked at her. "It's not very often that I get a pretty visitor like you."

Their rickshaw turned out of the station, the man standing up on the pedals to gain momentum. Pipra wasn't much of a town. Tricia had seen most of it from the train. They entered the one main street, a line of provision stores and general merchants, rickety buildings covered with signs and advertisements. People were seated in the shade of trees. The traffic on the street was mostly bicycles and rickshaws. Tricia felt precarious and exposed as they rode along. She could feel the rickshaw wobbling under their weight. A truck came roaring past, blaring its horn and sending the bicycles scattering to the sides. They passed a row of workshops at the side of the road. The intermittent bursts from a welding torch were even brighter than the sunlight. A man rode past on a bicycle with a block of ice strapped onto the carrier. Dr Fry waved to several people as they rode along. The rickshaw man was bathed in sweat. He was a gaunt man, all gristle and bone, and wore nothing but a torn pair of shorts and a grey singlet.

"I feel so guilty riding in this," said Tricia.

"Why's that?" asked Fry.

"I mean it's awful for us to be sitting back here while he works himself to death." She pointed to the rickshaw man. "All this weight . . . it doesn't seem fair."

"I would have come in the ambulance," said Fry, "but it's broken down and I haven't had a chance to work on it. She's a fifty-six Studebaker. Something's gone wrong with the fuel pump. Actually, I've come to the conclusion that a rickshaw is really a much more dependable form of transport. It's the perfect vehicle for these streets, sturdy, manœuvrable."

"Still, that doesn't make it right," said Tricia. Her nerves were on edge from the journey.

"I don't know," said Fry, seriously, the lines on his face converging.

"But, couldn't he get a horse and carriage instead," said Tricia. "Or something like that?"

"Then he'd have to feed the horse as well as himself and family."

Tricia shook her head, forcing herself to keep quiet. This was not the way she had wanted to begin her visit.

"I'm not saying it's the best solution," said Fry. "Or that it's a particularly good life being a rickshaw puller. I just admire the ingenuity of the guy who invented this thing."

The rickshaw man had settled back on his seat as they reached the open road on the other side of the town. He was now working the pedals with an easier motion. Dr Fry could sense that Tricia was upset and he tried to distract her by pointing out the landmarks, the district jail, the police lines, and the octroi barrier. There were trees on either side of the road, casting fluid shadows in the dust. Dr Fry pointed out the spire of the church in the distance. He began to tell her about the mission hospital, how it was founded in 1922 by Presbyterian missionaries from America. Tricia listened politely, as though she were interested, but all she really wanted to know was about herself.

As the rickshaw turned into the gate of the compound, Tricia could see what looked to her like an enormous pile of straw, a giant hayrick. Dr Fry had covered his bungalow with khus-khus tatties, a kind of thatch. The bhishti was on the roof, sprinkling the khus-khus with water.

"Here we are," said Fry, as the rickshaw came to a stop. Seeing the look of uncertainty in Tricia's eyes, he grinned. "Air-conditioning. The hot air blows through the wet grass and cools the house."

Tricia couldn't see a doorway and wondered what the house was going to be like inside. Two men had appeared from the back of the bungalow. They greeted Tricia cheerfully and unloaded the suitcases. She saw that Fry was reaching for his wallet to pay the rickshaw man and hurried to stop him.

"Please," she said. "Let me pay."

Fry tried to wave her off, but she insisted.

"How much?" she asked.

"Four or five rupees," said Fry.

She looked at him in astonishment.

"You're kidding," she said. "This man carried us all the way from the station with my suitcases. That's not even fifty cents."

"It's usually three rupees," said Fry. "I always give a little extra."

Tricia opened her purse, took out twenty rupees and handed it to the man. He looked at the note and shook his head.

"He won't have any change," said Fry.

"Tell him he can keep it," she said.

Dr Fry chewed his lip for a moment and then spoke to the rickshaw man, who took the twenty rupees reluctantly, turned it over in his hand and got back onto the rickshaw, without a word. Tricia felt ashamed of herself. She could see that Fry was embarrassed. Yet it mattered a great deal to her for some reason, to have given the money, even if the man hadn't made any gesture of thanks.

Dr Fry held one of the thatch curtains aside for Tricia to enter. Inside it was much cooler and the khus-khus gave off a musty fragrance. There was a verandah all along the front of the bungalow, which was empty except for a few pieces of broken furniture. They entered the main door into the dining room and Tricia looked up at the high ceilings. There were fans in each of the rooms, spinning slowly, which added to the feeling of airy emptiness. The floors were made of smooth bricks and the walls were white. There was a large table and a set of straight-backed chairs, plain and functional, a sideboard and several pictures on the walls. The living room was just as bare and neatly arranged, with an ascetic sense of order and simplicity. Because of the khus-khus, the rooms were in darkness and the air was moist. The only light came from the roshandans, small rectangular ventilators on a level with the ceiling, admitting narrow shafts of light which fell in geometric patterns on the wall.

Dr Fry led Tricia to her room. It was somewhat brighter than the rest of the bungalow, though the ceilings were still high and the furnishings were simple. There was a single bed in the middle of the room, covered with mosquito netting. The carved legs of the bed were set in bowls of water to keep the ants away. Her suitcases had been placed beside a dressing table with drawers which stood against one wall. There was a tall almira with a full-length mirror on the door.

"I'm afraid it's a little primitive," said Fry, apologizing. "But I think you'll be quite comfortable. Breakfast will be ready in a few minutes, as soon as you've washed up. The bathroom is right through there."

He left her alone and for a moment Tricia was afraid. The vacant spaces of the room, the mysterious odour of khus-khus, the silence

23

of the house, made her realize the distance she had come.

She opened the door of the bathroom and found it clean and bare. The toilet had an overhead tank and chain for flushing. There was a single tap on the wall, dripping into a bucket, also a tin tub lying on its side; no sink, but a wooden stand with a wash basin and a mug instead. A small mirror had been nailed to the wall. Tricia filled the basin with water and washed her face and hands. The towels were coarse and smelled of disinfectant. She desperately wanted a bath and to change her clothes but decided to wait until after breakfast. A movement on the wall startled her and she saw a gecko climbing up the pipes, a pale, tan-coloured creature with bulging eyes. It disappeared behind the cistern.

Back in the bedroom, Tricia opened one of the suitcases and felt beneath her clothes until she found the gift which she had brought for Dr Fry. She hadn't known what to get, searching through the men's departments at two or three stores without success. It made her realize how little she knew about him. She had wondered whether he smoked or drank, whether he wore ties and cuff links, running through the list of presents which she usually bought for Fritz on Fathers' day. Tricia had guessed that Dr Fry was a man of simple tastes. Nothing flashy. Something he could use, a practical gift, something which he wouldn't be able to get in India. The day before she left Hartford, Tricia went into a gift shop at the downtown Mall. The salesman had suggested a pocket knife and she had liked the idea immediately. It seemed to fit her image of Dr Fry. After looking through a whole range of knives, with different sized blades, corkscrews, can openers, screwdrivers, she finally chose an expensive model with an attachment for peeling potatoes. She had felt a touch of doubt after buying it, thinking she might have made a mistake, but now that she had met Dr Fry, Tricia knew that he would like the gift.

Tricia decided to open the second suitcase and check to see that everything was all right. Putting the case on the bed, she unlocked it and lifted out the carboard box which lay within. Opening the top, Tricia glanced inside to make sure that the pewter urn was still intact. Actually, it was probably stronger than the suitcase and tightly sealed, but Tricia had visions of the whole thing opening up and scattering ashes everywhere.

The urn contained the remains of her Aunt Penny who had once been the nursing superintendent at Pipra. Tricia had carried it back, in deference to Aunt Penny's wishes, so that she could be buried in the little town where she had worked. Even though Tricia was used to it by now, the presence of the urn gave her an uncomfortable feeling. On the aeroplane she had suddenly thought of what would happen if they asked her to open the urn at customs. They might even think that she was smuggling drugs and the idea of poor Aunt Penny being mistaken for a shipment of cocaine was horrifying and funny at the same time. Fortunately, when Tricia got off the plane in Delhi she didn't even have to open her bags at customs and they let her walk right through.

Closing the cardboard box, she put it carefully away in the cupboard, where it was out of sight. Whenever she touched the urn, Tricia felt as though she was performing a kind of ritual ceremony for the dead. She closed the cupboard hurriedly, shaking off a macabre sense of fear.

There was nobody in the living room when Tricia went out. She sat down in one of the easy chairs and flipped through an old issue of *National Georgaphic* which lay on the coffee table. The living and dining rooms were connected by an open archway. The lights had been turned on and Tricia could see that the table was set for breakfast. The cook entered with a jug of water. Through one of the doors behind her, another servant passed by in barefoot silence, carrying a mop and broom. Just like something out of Rudyard Kipling, she thought, the drab colonial bungalow, the dutiful retainers, the lack of modern amenities and yet a leisurely lifestyle, the comfort of bygone days. This was how a white man lived amongst the natives. . . .

Dr Fry came out of his bedroom, straightening the collar of his shirt and looking a little less dishevelled than before. He had shaved and combed his hair.

"Why don't we sit down at the table," he said. "I think Ghulam Rusool has breakfast ready."

Tricia got up and handed him the present. She had wrapped it in coloured paper.

"What's this?" he asked, puzzled.

"Just a little something," she said, feeling awkward. They seemed to share so much between them and yet they were strangers.

"For me?" he asked.

"I don't know whether you'll like it," she said, going around the end of the table, to take her seat. He opened the package carefully, trying to save the paper, but when he saw the knife in its cardboard box, he tore it open eagerly.

"I've always wanted one of these," he said. "Thank you."

Tricia smiled foolishly, not knowing what to say. He fondled the knife as if it were a toy and opened the larger blade, testing the edge on his thumb. One by one, he opened each of the parts, admiring the workmanship and the quality of the steel.

"I used to have an old jack-knife," he said, "but I lost it a couple of years ago. Of course it wasn't anything as special as this, just a single blade and a screwdriver. I'd had it since I was a boy and the blade had been sharpened so many times that I was sure it was going to snap. I'll have to look after this one carefully, make sure I don't lose it. Thanks a lot."

Tricia had noticed a plaque on the wall. It looked as though it was made of plaster of paris, painted in red and green, like some sort of cheap souvenir or Christmas decoration. It said: "Jesus Christ is the unseen guest, the head of this house, the silent listener at every conversation."

The cook entered with a bowl of cornflakes and set it down in front of Tricia. He was an old man. When he smiled, there were only four teeth in his mouth. Stepping back, he said something to her in Hindustani and laughed. Dr Fry looked up from the pocket knife and translated.

"Ghulam Rusool wants to know if you remember him. He's been with me for thirty years and helped take care of you, when you were small."

Tricia looked at the old cook, embarrassed. He had a round face with parched skin. His eyes were rheumy and moist as though he had been cutting onions.

She didn't know what to reply. Her jaws were beginning to ache from all this smiling, all this cheerfulness. The cook said something else and went back into the kitchen.

"What was that?" she asked.

"He said that you haven't been eating enough. You've hardly grown."

This time she laughed.

"Better have some cornflakes," he said, offering her the bowl.

"No thanks. I don't usually eat breakfast. I'll just have some tea if that's all right."

"The most important meal of the day," said Fry. He took the

bowl and helped himself, then sliced a banana over the top and flooded the cereal with milk. The table was laid with care, each jar and utensil in its proper place. The sugar bowl and pitcher of milk were covered with lace doilies, weighted with blue beads. Instead of a table cloth there were place mats, decorated with a palm tree and a camel. The colours had faded. There were cloth napkins in wooden rings and the tea cups were turned upside down in their saucers. The knitted tea-cosy which had come unravelled at the bottom fitted snuggly over the pot, the white spout sticking out as if it were the trunk of an elephant. Tricia helped herself to tea and drank it without sugar or milk.

"How was your trip?" asked Fry.

"Exhausting," she said. "I'm glad it's over."

"I don't know about you, but the jet lag usually kills me. It takes at least a week to recover." He glanced at his watch. "Let's see, right now it's just about ten o'clock at night in Hartford."

And I'd be watching TV with Fritz and Sally, she thought, a peculiar feeling of displacement coming over her.

"I hate flying," said Fry. "It's no way to travel."

"But it sure gets you where you want to go," she said, "I still can't believe I'm halfway around the world."

Fry spooned the sodden cornflakes into his mouth, leaning forward over the bowl, so that he wouldn't spill.

"We used to always travel by ship in the old days," he said, "P & O, Cunard, the French and Italian lines. It was marvellous. There's nothing to do on a ship but relax."

"When did you stop coming by ship?" she asked.

"I sailed on one of the last P & O liners in fifty-eight, but before that I'd flown in one of those boat planes," he said.

"A boat plane?" she said.

"The strangest looking airplane you've ever seen, with two big pontoons instead of wheels and three propellers. It was tied up at the end of this dock in Southampton and made an awful racket starting up. The gulls were terrified. I remember feeling the plane rocking on the water before we took off, the waves slopping over the pontoons. We seemed to skid over the surface until the plane lifted off. It was the weirdest sensation. We puddle-jumped across the Mediteranean; breakfast in Gibraltar, lunch in Malta, then spent the night in Cyprus at a hotel. The next morning we were off to Suez and Aden, following the coast to some place in the Gulf,

27

then on to Karachi, where we spent the second night. I still remember flying into Bombay and splashing down near the gateway of India."

"How often do you go back to the States?" asked Tricia.

"Once every three years. At least that's what I'm supposed to do; it used to be once in five, for a full year's furlough. Now we have these three month furloughs, which is nicer. A year's too long to be away from Pipra."

"Where do you go in the States?" she asked.

"I've got a brother in Kansas. He's a minister there. I also have to visit each of the churches which support the hospital. Mostly I spend the time travelling around. I rent a car or go by Greyhound, usually. Then of course, a lot of old friends from the mission field are settled in America, in retirement homes."

Tricia imagined him riding a Greyhound senicruiser. She wondered whether he always wore shorts. He looked a little like a boy scout, she thought, collecting merit badges, helping old ladies across the street, whittling sticks with his jackknife. There was an innocence about him, part of a lost America, which Tricia had never known but always imagined existed, the midwestern farm boy, paper routes, cornflakes and Sunday school, that boyish sense of optimism. She could almost picture him chewing on a stem of grass as he floated down the Mississippi.

"Have you brought the ashes?" asked Dr Fry.

"Yes," said Tricia, turning her napkin ring around one finger.

"I've spoken to Padre Massey and we've decided to have the service on Wednesday afternoon, day after tomorrow."

"That's fine. I guess there isn't any rush," said Tricia.

Fry took another spoonful of cornflakes and hesitated before he swallowed.

"Miss Reynolds was a dedicated woman," said Fry. "Very professional. The best nursing superintendent I've ever known. She had our hospital running like a Swiss watch."

"I was never very close to her," said Tricia, "though she used to visit us when I was young and we'd go down to see her in the retirement home in Philadelphia."

They both were silent for a moment as if out of respect for the dead. Fry pushed his empty bowl aside.

"And your parents," he said, "how are they?"

"They're fine," said Tricia. "You never met them, did you?"

"Nope. I spoke with them on the phone a couple of times."

Tricia felt as though they had so much to talk about and yet they could not get beyond small-talk. Fry kept his eyes on the place mat. Ghulam Rusool brought toast in a wire rack, which he put down on the table.

"You want eggs?" he said, trying his English.

"No thank you," said Tricia.

Ghulam Rusool looked disapprovingly from her to Fry and then said something in Hindustani.

"He says that if you don't eat anything, you're never going to grow up."

"I'll have a piece of toast," she said.

The cook turned and left. Tricia took a slice and broke it in two.

"Sometime, I'd like you to tell me the whole story," said Tricia. "Who was my mother? How it happened? Everything."

"Well, I'm afraid there isn't very much to tell," said Dr Fry.

"Fritz and Sally explained a little bit. But I think they didn't really want to know the facts."

"I suppose that's only natural," he said.

"Yes, maybe," said Tricia. "Was I born at this hospital?"

"No. Your mother brought you here when you were two or three months old. You were very sick, dysentery and dehydration. For a while it was touch and go. We didn't think that you would live. But in the end you did pull through."

Dr Fry was silent for a while, his memory clouding over. Sometimes it seemed to have happened just the day before and at other times the memory was so distant.

"Did my mother just leave me at the hospital and go away?"

"No," said Fry, "she stayed with us for six or seven months. One of the women on the compound gave her a room to live in. I don't think she had anywhere to go. Her husband had died."

"My father?" said Tricia.

"She never called him that," said Fry. "I remember that she didn't like to speak about her family. The nurses tried to ask her questions but she never told them much."

"What was her name?"

"Mamta," said Fry. "She was a tribal woman and probably came from somewhere in the hills."

"How old would she have been?" asked Tricia.

"Fifteen, sixteen at the most. Just a girl," said Fry.

"And she was a widow, at that age?" said Tricia, in disbelief.

"She was probably married when she was very young, eight or nine," said Fry. "There are laws against that sort of thing but it happens all the time."

"What would have made her go away?" asked Tricia.

Fry shook his head, staring down at the tablecloth.

"It's hard to say. Nobody expected her to leave. She had even decided to become a Christian. I don't know what made her change her mind. It could have been that she was frightened."

"Frightened of what?" said Tricia.

Dr Fry seemed to hesitate.

"Well, it's very difficult for a woman living on her own," he said. "She has no security."

"Couldn't she have married someone else? I mean, she was so young," said Tricia.

"It would have been difficult. Widows have a certain stigma as it is and with a daughter, it would be very hard to find a husband," said Fry.

"Maybe she just wanted to start her life all over again," said Tricia.

"We tried to find out where she'd gone and had to report the matter to the police, which always scares people off. The news spread quickly all over town but nobody could trace her."

Fry grinned, trying to soften the impact for her, but Tricia had already hardened herself to the facts. She tried to force a smile to reassure him. It seemed to hurt Fry more, retelling the story, than for her to hear it.

"And what about me?" asked Tricia.

"We kept you at the hospital for a week or two. All the nurses were in love with you. A cheerful baby, with a loud voice and very determined to get whatever you wanted."

"But I couldn't have been the only orphan you've had to deal with," she said.

"Of course not. We often get foundlings and sometimes older children who've lost their parents. Sometimes it happens that a woman gives birth and doesn't want the child, either she's unmarried, or some such reason . . ."

"What do you do with them?"

"The church has several orphanages. We often send them there, or sometimes to the government homes."

30

"But you didn't send me to an orphanage," said Tricia.

Fry smiled at her, with a mischievous look.

"No, I didn't," he said.

"Why not?"

"I don't know . . . I guess I liked you." He shrugged, buttering a toast. Tricia had crumbled part of hers between her fingers but hadn't eaten it.

"You kept me for almost a year," said Tricia.

"Ten months. I had to hire an ayah, a nanny to change your diapers and wash you. I wasn't very good at that."

"But something made you change your mind," said Tricia.

Fry scratched his eyebrow with embarrassment.

"Yes, I guess so," said Fry. "For a while I thought I might adopt you, but I realized that it wouldn't work."

"How come?"

"Well, I hadn't really thought things through. It's a big responsibility, taking on a child."

"I suppose Aunt Penny helped dissuade you."

"Yes, she didn't think it was the proper thing to do, a single man trying to raise a daughter on his own," said Fry with an inward smile.

"She wrote to Fritz and Sally about me and they wrote back to you. That's how it all happened, right?"

"Something like that. Miss Reynolds recommended them very highly. By that time I was beginning to wonder what I was going to do with you. They couldn't have any children, as I remember, and wanted to adopt a baby very badly."

"Yes, Sally kept having miscarriages," said Tricia.

"It took such a long time to process the papers," said Fry. "We had to get it sanctioned through the local courts, which is like pulling teeth, umpteen different forms and affidavits. The red tape was incredible. Then the US Embassy in Delhi had to issue papers, which took some time."

It was almost as though they were talking about someone else now and not Tricia herself. Fry's hand kept returning to the pocket knife beside his plate, turning it around, touching it, feeling the smoothness of the steel.

"Miss Reynolds was going back on furlough and she took you with her to the States. I didn't envy her, travelling with a year-old baby. In those days it used to take almost forty-eight hours to fly from Delhi to New York."

"It must have been very difficult," said Tricia.

He glanced up at her.

"Sending me away like that," she said.

Fry stared at the knuckles of his hand, Tricia noticed there was a gold wedding band on his finger.

"I felt very lonely afterwards," he said. "For a couple of months I would wake up listening for your crying in the night, but I knew that you would get a much better life in America . . . "

Tricia kept her eyes on him.

"Do you really mean that?" she asked.

"Yes," he said, with conviction. "I mean, imagine what it would have been like for you growing up in a place like Pipra. It would have been awfully boring. Or worse, if you'd been sent to one of those orphanages."

Tricia took a sip of her tea and said nothing.

"Once or twice I thought of coming to see you in the States," said Fry, "while I was on furlough, but something always popped up and I wasn't able to make it."

"Conveniently," said Tricia.

Fry smiled at her and looked away.

Ghulam Rusool came in with a plate of scrambled eggs and fresh toast. He put it down in front of Fry and scowled at Tricia's plate. She had nibbled a corner of the crust, that was all.

"I'm really not very hungry this morning," she said, apologizing.

Fry put ketchup on his scrambled eggs. She wondered whether he always ate alone in this room at the large teak table, under the high ceilings. For a moment it was as though she were not there. He was crouched over his plate, one shoulder higher than the other. Tricia felt as though she was the unseen guest, watching him eat the meal by himself.

FOUR

AFTER BREAKFAST, Dr Fry went back to the hospital, leaving Tricia to bathe and unpack her things. He told her to come across around eleven o'clock when he would start his rounds. That way he could show her the hospital at the same time. Having had three cups of tea, Fry felt revived, though his back was worse than ever. He couldn't stop thinking about Tricia, her voice, her mannerisms, her face, her hands. She seemed a little too serious about life, he thought, but there was nothing wrong with that. How strange it must be for her, to come all this way and find a town like Pipra. He tried to imagine what she was thinking.

Fry had always known that she would return. A week ago he had been washing up after surgery when Gyani brought in the mail. There were the usual magazines and journals, bills and circulars. Fry noticed the corner of the airmail envelope sticking out of the pile. He never got much personal mail. His fingers were still damp when he took the letter out and looked at the unfamiliar handwriting. Flipping it over, he saw the address: Tricia Crawford, 18 Adams Lane, West Hartford, Ct, USA 06843. For a moment he was puzzled until the name registered in his mind. If she had written Patricia instead, he would have known who it was immediately. In his eagerness, he tore the letter while opening the envelope and had to piece it together on his desk.

Dear Dr Fry,

I don't know whether you remember who I am. I was born in India sometime during the summer of 1960. I am an orphan and you took care of me until I was adopted by Fritz and Sally Crawford.

My Aunt Penny used to be the nursing superintendent at your hospital. I am sure you've heard that she died last month in her retirement home. One of the requests which she made in her will was that her ashes be buried in Pipra. I've decided that I'll bring them to India myself. For a long time I've wanted to visit my birthplace and I probably won't get another chance to make the trip. I wonder if you would mind

33

arranging for the burial. We've already had a memorial service so it only needs to be a simple ceremony. I'm sorry to bother you, but I know you'll understand.

This trip means a great deal to me. I finished college this summer and I'm trying to decide what to do with my life. India seems to be such an important part of me and yet I've never seen the place. I'm looking forward to meeting you. Aunt Penny told me all about your work and I'm sure we have a lot to talk about.

I plan to reach India on the 3rd of September and catch a train as soon as possible, hopefully the same day. I haven't been able to find Pipra on any of the maps but I imagine it's still there.

With all good wishes and special thanks.
Yours sincerely,
Tricia Crawford

He had laughed out loud at the polite hesitancy of the letter, then realized that the third of September was the day after tomorrow. Her letter had taken twenty days to reach Pipra. Dr Fry was usually a quiet man with plenty of self-control, but after reading the letter, he couldn't stop grinning at himself in the mirror as he dried his hands.

Later, that same evening after supper, he had become more subdued and began to make plans for Tricia's visit. Fry tried hard to imagine what she would look like and got out a picture which was taken shortly before she left for the States. He was holding her, looking a great deal younger. Tricia was nothing more than a small bundle of clothes and a serious little face.

When Mamta ran away and left the girl, most people, the hospital staff and his mission colleagues had assumed that she would be sent to an orphanage in the hills, where they kept children in blue uniforms and taught them Bible along with their other classes until the age of eighteen. He tried to picture what Tricia might have looked like if she'd been sent up there. She'd have called me "Uncle", he thought, and worn her hair in ribbons. Nobody had wanted him to keep the child. He could remember how it had bothered the other missionaries, as well as the Indian Christians. They doubted that he could look after and care for a young girl by himself. Miss Reynolds, a real battle-axe, whom he still recalled

34

with mixed feelings, had finally taken the matter into her own hands. She was a spinster, whom everyone feared. She'd been with the red cross during the second world war before joining the mission as nursing superintendent, and always spoke to him as though he were a wounded GI.

"A kid needs both a mother and a father," she said, chewing the words as though her mouth were full of bubble gum. "A real family, Gene. People like you and me have to realize that we're loners. We can't ever hope to bring up children properly. It wouldn't be fair on the poor kid."

He had wanted to say that she was being unfair, assuming that he was a loner like herself, but Dr Fry had finally given in. Much as he would have liked to keep the baby, he decided that she should be sent to America. Now, of course, he wasn't so sure.

After he got word that Miss Reynolds had died Dr Fry had put up a photograph of her in the nursing station, feeling somehow that it was the least he could do for a woman who had been selfless in her service to the hospital, while at the same time being one of the most selfish persons he had known. She didn't want anyone else to have those pleasures in life which she had denied herself.

Tricia decided not to use the tin tub and took a bath from the bucket instead, squatting down on the floor and pouring the tepid water over herself with the mug. There was a hole in the corner of the bathing area, where the water drained out. She washed her hair and filled the bucket again halfway. Holding it above her head, she let the water cascade over her body. Instead of drying herself with the coarse towels, she went into the bedroom still dripping wet and stood under the fan. The evaporation cooled her and she felt as though she had washed away all of the dirt and grime from the train journey.

Tricia saw herself naked in the almira mirror and stared for a moment at the boyish figure, the dark skin. A boyfriend had once called her "tadpole" and now she realized how it applied to her, an unformed, embryonic woman. This is her, she thought, my mother's image in which I am created.

Fritz and Sally had explained that she was adopted as soon as she was old enough to understand. Not that she hadn't noticed, since even at that age it was fairly obvious to her that she was a different colour from her parents. Fritz was a stockbroker and for the first five years of her life in America they had lived in Manhattan. Tricia still had a faded picture in her mind of the apartment, the cast-iron radiators and the black doorman who used to let her ride the elevators all day long.

The Crawfords moved to Connecticut when Tricia turned six. Fritz got a job in Hartford with a bank. She could remember the enormous yellow truck with a picture of a green sailing ship and MAYFLOWER written across the side of the trailer. They had bought a house in West Hartford, where Tricia began her suburban childhood. The first day they moved in, she stood on the flagstones of the patio and stared at the lawn, the sward of green, as smooth as a carpet, not a dandelion or weed to mar its perfect surface. Hesitantly, she stepped onto the lawn, felt it give under her feet and then lay down, each blade of grass piercing her with a sensation of nervous excitement. There were trees behind the house, maples and spruce, a bird bath at which the cardinals and squirrels congregated. Having lived most of her life on the twelfth floor, Tricia found it strange to wake up in the mornings and look outside, to see the ground immediately beneath her window. Of course she missed the doorman and some of her friends from the apartment house, but there was such a sense of freedom in her new surroundings, she felt no loneliness. They had moved at the end of July and there was still a month of summer before she had to attend first grade. Part of the reason why they had left New York was that Fritz and Sally had been afraid to send her to the public schools in Manhattan. Tricia was enrolled at the elementary school in West Hartford and began riding the yellow buses each morning. The school was a solid, grandiose building which had eventually been declared a fire trap and closed. On her last visit, she had noticed that it had been torn down and replaced by a retirement home.

Their house in West Hartford was a modern split-level with a rock garden in front and a mail box in the shape of a barn. Fritz had bought a station wagon as the family car and a second-hand Thunderbird for himself. Sally began collecting green stamps. In those days Sally seemed happy and satisfied, the way she hummed Cole Porter to herself as she tossed a salad or strolled the aisles of the A & P, selecting the weekly specials from the loaded shelves. There was no hint of sadness, no pain in her smile. She had brought Tricia up to be a well-mannered, sensitive child.

Sally always made her finish the food on her plate. If Tricia ever wasted anything, Sally would tell her that there were people starving in India who'd make a meal of what she threw away. It was really the only time her mother mentioned India and Tricia grew up imagining a place where people ate leftovers scraped from children's plates. Sometimes she wondered whether Sally meant it as a reminder that she herself could easily have been one of those starving people.

Fritz and Sally never liked to talk about India, partly because they knew so little about her past but also because they wanted to pretend that Tricia was a child of their own. They did not hide the truth from her but at the same time they did not force it on her, playing the happy charade, pretending that she was their real daughter. Tricia could remember how Fritz always told her that she had inherited his nose and Sally's eyes. It was almost a joke, but not quite, and he used to tell it far too often.

For a while Tricia made believe that she was a red Indian like Pocohontas, living in a teepee – an Indian princess taken captive by the pioneers. There were deeper fantasies which never quite expressed themselves, images of tropical forests and pagan rituals, a primitive world of natural shapes and shadows. It was something beyond memory as though her imagination conjured up a mythical India, her own vision of what might have been. The uncertainty of her dreams left Tricia feeling naked and abandoned. Sometimes she heard voices soughing in the darkness but as soon as she tried to hear what they were saying, all was silent.

Tricia had grown up with the knowledge that she was a fortunate child, rescued from a life of deprivation and suffering. When people looked at her they seemed to be thinking, what a lucky girl, and though she always tried to show her gratitude it was never quite enough, never enough to pay back the debt. She felt as though there was something dishonest about her escape from poverty, something sinful and perverse, as though she had betrayed a part of herself. She had a Christian name but sometimes it felt as though it wasn't her own. She had got it by mistake, through some quirk of circumstance. Tricia had always lived in doubt and fear, waiting for the moment when she would be sent back, rejected like a misfit shoe or blouse that didn't quite match. She was always aware that her parents' love was tenuous. There was something false about her mother's touch, her father's kiss. As she grew up, Tricia began to realize the tension in their marriage, the binding structure of a family in which she was the weak link, the uncertain knot.

From the beginning Tricia had insisted on calling her parents Fritz and Sally, instead of Mom and Dad. They didn't seem to mind and she hadn't thought anything of it, until some of her friends said that she was weird. Nobody else in school seemed to call their parents by their first names, but then of course, nobody else in school was adopted. Fritz and Sally they had remained and even now she couldn't separate their names. It was like one of those catchy phrases on a billboard, 'Fritz 'n Sally'. The names stuck together in her mind even though she knew they belonged apart.

After her bath, Tricia dressed herself in the coolest clothes she'd brought and headed outside towards the hospital. The sun was almost directly overhead. There were no shadows at all, except under the darkest trees. A group of children were playing marbles near the gate. Tricia paused to watch but they looked up at her with uncertainty and stopped their game abruptly. Tricia hurried across the road, through the gate of the hospital. The entrance to the hospital was dark and smelled of formaldehyde. The man at the door stood up and saluted.

Tricia hated hospitals, the atmosphere of cloistered infirmity. Only once in her life had she been admitted, when she'd had her tonsils out. That time she had wanted to escape the white walls and sheets, the soundproof ceilings, the soap operas on the TV and the nurses in their white uniforms and fruity lipstick. She hated to be sick and even more to be treated as though she were sick, a contagious, contaminating presence.

"Where can I find Dr Fry?" she asked.

The man at the door pointed ahead and she went down a long hallway, with doors on either side, each with a sign – Laboratory, X–ray, Chapel, Nurse's Station. The smell of disinfectant was asphyxiating. The halls were gloomy and narrow. Tricia could vaguely make out the shapes of people sitting on the benches in the shadows. The hospital was larger than she had thought, with connecting passages and courtyards leading off into different wings. At the end of the hall there was an open door and a sign for the Out-Patients Department. A large rectangular room, with benches along the walls, opened out onto another verandah. The doctors were seated in a row, each with a chair and table.

Dr Fry was examining a woman's throat. He had a flashlight held between his teeth, so that both his hands were free. In one he held a tongue depresser and in the other a cotton swab, with which he was taking a throat culture. Not wanting to interrupt, Tricia stood in the doorway and watched. After he had finished with the woman, Fry examined a child with an infected hand. He spoke softly to the child as he unwrapped the bandage. Each of the patients waiting in the room or on the verandah had their eyes trained on him. The nurses circulated amongst them, checking their temperatures, noting it down on the patient's card and then shaking the thermometers with an efficient flick of their wrists and putting them back in a beaker filled with yellow solution. Children howled from time to time but there was a silence in the room, as if some kind of ceremony were under way.

After Tricia had been standing in the doorway for several minutes, Dr Fry glanced over his shoulder and saw her. He finished with the patient he was examining and then got up from his chair painfully and came across to where she was standing.

"You should have told me you were here," he said.

"I didn't want to interrupt," she said.

As Dr Fry led the way down the hall, a man came scurrying out of a door marked, "Accounts" and handed Fry a clipboard on which there were a number of vouchers. Without looking at these, Fry took the pen from his shirt pocket and signed them each with an illegible scrawl, giving the clipboard back to the accountant with a nod. He seemed unhurried but distracted, a little impatient.

"Why don't we start at the nursery," he said.

"Please," said Tricia, "I'm sure you've got your routines. I don't want to upset your schedule."

"Oh, I gave up following a schedule long ago," he said. "I used to try but it means you're always looking at a clock and not getting anything done. Besides, the nursery is always the most cheerful place to begin, helps me face the rest of the day."

He pushed open a swinging door and politely held it open for her to go inside, as though they were entering a restaurant for dinner.

"We actually don't get that many maternity cases," he said, "unless there are complications. The midwives handle most of the deliveries at home and seem to do a fairly good job, though their sense of hygiene leaves something to be desired and you still can't convince them that it isn't necessary to put cowdung on the umbilical cord for it to heal."

A baby was crying loudly and Dr Fry stopped beside the crib. Two nurses had followed them into the room, carrying charts and Fry's stethoscope which he had forgotten in OPD.

Dr Fry introduced them to Tricia and the nurses nodded shyly.

As he began to examine the infants, Fry casually picked up one of the babies and coddled it for a moment, then handed the child to Tricia. The baby was no more than a few hours old and felt as though it weighed nothing, eyes pinched together, one hand lifted in sleep, the tiny fingers opening and closing. Tricia had never held a baby in her life before. She felt awkward and afraid. One of the nurses moved her arm to a more comfortable position and Tricia tried to rock the baby. She had never been very good with children and always found them to be so helpless. Fry took his time checking on the other children while Tricia stood there stiffly, the baby sound asleep in her arms. Fry had given it to her without any explanation, almost as if it were a gift.

The weightlessness of the child frightened her as she realized how fragile its bones must be, the skin nothing more than a translucent membrane. She could easily have crushed the baby in her arms. What startled her also was the colour, a bluish grey with a shock of black hair. Somehow, she had always imagined babies to be pink. Tricia looked at her own hand, a darker brown but still the same colour. She tried to recognize herself in the child but couldn't. The baby was not hers. She had dreamt of having children but in those dreams she always gave birth to pale, unsightly creatures. Tricia had decided that she would never make a good mother. She had no maternal instincts. She would be like one of those lions in the zoo she'd read about, that ate their own cubs.

"A boy," said Fry, coming back to her. "We had to do a caesarian. His mother's just recovering. Babies need to be held. It's good for them."

One of the nurses took the child and put it back in the crib. They left the maternity ward through another door and crossed a verandah which was lined with beds.

"You don't seem to have many empty beds," said Tricia.

"I doubt if we've had an empty bed for the last ten years. There are always patients that we have to treat in OPD and send back home, who really should be hospitalized."

"How do you decide?" she asked.

"Well, it usually depends on how badly off they are and

sometimes how far they've come. You can't send a critical case back home if that means eight hours by bullock cart," Fry said. "We try to move our patients out as soon as possible. Nobody stays here any longer than they need to."

"How many doctors do you have?" she asked.

"Not enough," said Fry. "There are three of us and one intern. The most difficult thing about this hospital is keeping staff. Nobody wants to live in a place like Pipra. They keep complaining that there isn't any life in this town. I don't blame them really. It must get pretty dull at times and I guess there aren't many prospects here, no future for an ambitious young person."

There was a man mopping the floor and he saluted Fry as they stepped around the bucket of grey water which smelled strongly of disinfectant.

"Now we can go to the general ward," said Fry. "There are a couple of patients that I want to check on."

The two nurses led the way through another swinging door and Tricia found herself in a long room lined with beds. Here and there white cloth screens had been set up around a bed, where the patient needed privacy. Dr Fry disappeared behind one of these. Tricia waited outside, listening to him speaking in muted voice, to which there was no reply. When he came out, he blinked at her. With methodical patience he went down the row of beds studying the charts on each, asking questions of the nurses, making a notation, checking a woman's eyes or respiration. For Tricia it all seemed so crowded and pitiful, seeing the gaunt faces of the women, hearing them cough. She couldn't stand the sight of pain or suffering. It was only Dr Fry's presence which kept her from running out of the room.

Tricia noticed a peculiar scene at the end of the ward. There seemed to be a man pedalling a bicycle, or something like a bicycle, except it was stationary. Her curiosity was almost too much for her, but she waited until they reached the last bed and Dr Fry turned to his invention and the girl who lay inside.

Her eyes were open now but she stared at those around her without recognition or understanding. Dr Fry brushed his hand across her forehead to calm the girl and inspected the tube in her throat. He glanced up at Tricia.

"Polio," he said.

"What's this for?" asked Tricia, pointing to the drum.

"It's an iron lung, to help her breathe."

"Where did you get it from?"

"I made it," he said.

Tricia shook her head in disbelief.

"I'd read about one with a hand-operated lever, but I figured your arm must get awfully tired," he said.

"Do you think she'll be all right?" asked Tricia.

Dr Fry curled his lip with a look of uncertainty.

"It's touch and go. If she makes it through this week, I think she'll recover, whatever that means. The disease is bound to cripple her, but it's hard to tell what kind of damage it will do."

Tricia met the girl's eyes with hers. Fry had moved on to the next bed. He had the whole length of the ward to complete, but Tricia stayed beside the iron lung. She tried hard to penetrate the glassy expression of fear on the girl's face. The man on the bicycle had his back to them and the pedals were squeaking. The machine looked more like a torture rack than a life-support device. Tricia touched the girl's cheek and again their eyes connected. She did not seem to be in pain. Tricia wanted desperately to do something for the girl, to feed her, to wash her face and brush her hair, anything that did not mean walking away. She thought of asking the man to get down and she would pedal for awhile, anything to help, anything but to stand there mute and helpless. Yet, that was all the girl seemed to want, to have someone to watch, someone she could fix in her stare. Tricia wished she could pick the girl up in her arms and hold her as she had done with the baby.

FIVE

THE GRAVEYARD was a walled enclosure on the far western corner of the compound. In fact, it was almost like a miniature compound in itself. There were only two trees, a very tall eucalyptus with a peeling trunk and a stunted kikad tree partly covered by a parasitic vine which was a sulphurous yellow. There was nobody at the graveyard and the gate was closed. Dr Fry had brought the key but it took some time to open the lock. Inside, there was a scattering of graves. Most of them had simple headstones and there was only one in the shape of a cross. Tricia could remember the cemetry where Sally's parents had been buried, several acres of rolling hills, covered with marble dominoes. She hated the feeling of the place, the quiet lawns and wilted wreaths. But the Pipra graveyard, this compound of the dead, was much more stark and cruel. The grass was sparse and withered. The only flash of colour was the yellow vine, like a creeping flame slowly devouring the kidad tree.

"It's not a very cheerful place," said Fry, as though he'd read her thoughts.

"Well, I'm sure Aunt Penny knew what she wanted," said Tricia. Fry nodded.

"There isn't much room in here any more," he said, picking his way around the graves, to a place near the eucalyptus tree.

Tricia followed him to the spot, feeling an uncomfortable sensation. It was almost as though they were laying out a summer garden, deciding where to plant the beans and carrots.

"That grave right there is Ruth's," he said. "You knew about Ruth didn't you?"

"Yes, Aunt Penny told me what happened," said Tricia softly.

With his toe, Dr Fry made a mark on the ground. He looked at Tricia hesitantly.

"I figured she'd like to be buried here, beside Ruth," said Fry. He seemed anxious for her approval.

"Of course," she said. "It's fine."

"I figure they don't need to dig too large a grave, just a pit, say eighteen inches across, big enough for the urn. We can lay the stone

43

like this," he said, using his heel to scrape a line in the dust. "And they can dig right here, maybe four feet down."

Fry seemed to have already worked out the exact dimensions of the grave, as though it became much easier when things were reduced to inches and feet. Tricia was hardly listening. She knelt down beside the nearby stone. It was a simple marble plaque, set in a slab of grey cement. The lettering had been chiselled into the stone. Tricia read the inscription to herself:

RUTH EMMANUEL
Born April 2, 1940   Died October 16, 1958

Fry had made his marks in the dust and stopped when he saw that Tricia was kneeling down, almost in an attitude of prayer.

"What about a stone?" she said. "I hadn't thought of that."

"We can order one from Indore," said Fry. "That's probably the best place to get it. You can decide on the inscription, if you like, and I can do that for you. It will take a couple of months."

"I wouldn't know what to say," said Tricia. "You'll have to help me choose a Bible verse."

Tricia wondered to herself whether Dr Fry would want to be buried here in this lifeless patch of earth. She could tell that the kikad tree was dying. The names on the gravestones were mostly Biblical, Indian Christians and those few missionaries who had died in Pipra. The brick walls were bleached with cancerous patches of white lime. A flock of parakeets came flying overhead, like a fusilade of green arrows. A bus roared past and Tricia thought how much the gravestones looked like the kilometre markers on the roadside, as if inscribed with distances instead of epitaphs. Tricia felt an overpowering sense of negative space and dislocation, like a figure in a surrealist landscape. She stared at the yellow vine with its sinuous tentacles that were slowly smothering the tree.

During the last twelve years of her life, Aunt Penny lived in a retirement home for missionaries in Philadelphia. Tricia and her parents would go to visit her once or twice a year and Fritz would phone her every Sunday evening. Earlier, when Tricia was still in elementary school, Aunt Penny would come and stay with them in

Hartford for a month or two, from Thanksgiving through Christmas. Tricia remembered how she stayed in the spare room at the end of the hall and always left her razor above the sink. She would travel by train and usually arrived with one large suitcase that Fritz could hardly carry. Aunt Penny had always seemed a forceful but kindly woman and Tricia enjoyed her visits. She would read stories to Tricia and go for walks with her around the neighbourhood. She was strict, of course, and if Tricia stayed awake beyond her bedtime, Aunt Penny was sure to make a remark. Once, she made her turn off the television while she was watching Saturday morning cartoons, saying that there were better things to do than strain your eyes watching Daffy Duck. Tricia had obeyed. It wasn't until many years later that Tricia realized how much Sally hated these visits. Aunt Penny had a way of taking over the house. When she thought back on it, Tricia could remember Aunt Penny saying something at the dinner table and Sally would look as though she was going to cry. After Tricia went into fifth grade, Aunt Penny had a fall and she was never able to travel again.

The retirement home was a grey apartment building not far from the Liberty Bell. There were plenty of other missionaries there as well, from all over the world, China, Thailand, Burma, Africa and South America. Aunt Penny said she liked it there because there were so many people like herself. They had a chapel in the basement and a dining hall, so that nobody had to do their own cooking, and though she complained about the food sometimes, it was a secure and comfortable place. They had doctors and nurses in attendance all day long and little call buttons in the rooms, which she could press in an emergency. The hairdresser would come once a week and the chiropodist to manicure her toe nails. Nobody had to leave the apartment building unless they wanted to. After her fall, in which she fractured her hip, Aunt Penny seemed more chastened and subdued. Fritz would insist on taking her out for a meal whenever they visited, but she was much happier giving them dinner in the dining hall. Tricia could remember standing in the line at the cafeteria, holding plastic trays, just like lunchtime at school; missionaries from different ends of the earth queuing up for hamburger steaks with gravy and mashed potatoes. They had lived such exciting lives, in places that most people could never pronounce. Yet, here they returned to the obscurity of a drab apartment house.

Aunt Penny never seemed unhappy at the retirement home and was always glad to see them when they drove down to Philadelphia. Sally hated these visits and said so openly, calling the home a living morgue. Fritz would argue when she said such things and the long drives to Philadelphia and back to Hartford were usually full of recriminations and bitterness. Tricia would sit in the back, with the seat belt wrapped tightly around her waist, half listening to her parents and watching the freeways slither past. At some point, Sally would say something like, "You'll never catch me living in a place like that."

Then Fritz would say, "Would you rather she lived with us?"

Sally would snap at him and pretty soon, Fritz would punch the buttons on the radio and they would fall silent to the wailing melodies of country western singers and dashboard serenades.

Aunt Penny was Fritz's mother's younger sister and the only surviving member of his family, except for distant cousins in Nebraska. He was close to her in a peculiar, dependent sort of way – an attachment which had developed only in his later years. He treated Aunt Penny with respect and she was obviously proud of her nephew and his affection for her. Fritz would spend most of their visits advising her about investments. Aunt Penny would listen attentively, but she refused to let him handle her money and always said that she was quite happy keeping her savings in Government bonds. There was so little of it anyway.

Tricia was sure that age had mellowed Aunt Penny and she could imagine her as a stern and abrasive woman. She was religious in a practical, conservative sort of way. Her opinions were rooted in the prairie soil of Nebraska where she had been born. She believed in hard work and common sense, though Tricia knew there was a darker side to her as well, the shadows of spinsterhood. Aunt Penny would show her disapproval about a lot of things and she was never happy about the way the Fritz and Sally treated Tricia. She did not approve of chewable vitamins. She did not approve of TV. She did not approve of Unitarians. Despite all that, however, she was very tolerant of Tricia herself and treated her with special fondness.

It was only after Tricia was in college that Sally had admitted how much she hated Aunt Penny. There had always been a rivalry between them, a clash of loyalties. Aunt Penny treated Sally as Fritz's wife and nothing else. She tended to blame Sally for never pushing her nephew hard enough to make a success in his career.

Aunt Penny believed that Fritz could have risen to the top of any bank if he had married an ambitious, aggressive woman. The problem of children only added to her disappointment and being a nurse she would sit and discuss the matter in detail, treating Sally as nothing but an anatomy lesson. Once, she had even examined her and Sally said that she had never felt herself as thoroughly violated as when Aunt Penny was probing about her cervix.

She was really a woman of contradictions, who liked to control the lives of people whom she loved. One moment, she would be sharp and domineering and a few minutes later, complain about the pain in her hip and act as helpless as a child.

About two years ago, when the family went down to visit her, Aunt Penny told Tricia the story of Ruth. Fritz and Sally had gone to visit some other friends in Philadelphia and left Tricia at the retirement home for the afternoon. They were sitting in Aunt Penny's room, an L–shaped apartment with a bed in one corner. The room was fairly plain, except for two enormous rosewood elephants on either side of the door and photographs from India on the walls.

Aunt Penny hardly ever spoke about India and even the pictures on the walls and the elephants seemed to belong to someone else. Tricia had never really questioned her about Pipra. Usually Fritz and Sally were also there and the whole situation was too awkward to raise the subject. But on that particular afternoon, when they were sitting alone together, Tricia felt as though Aunt Penny might be willing to talk.

"Do you ever want to go back to India?" asked Tricia.

Aunt Penny looked at her with a severe expression.

"You know I couldn't make the trip," she said. "Not in my condition."

"But you must have lots of memories," said Tricia.

"Some," she said, tilting her head to one side. "There's a lot of it that I wouldn't miss at all, the flies, the filth, the silly superstitions, but those are little things. I guess, sometimes I miss the dust storms and the poinsettias, the parakeets."

"I want to visit India some time," said Tricia.

Aunt Penny nodded.

"Don't expect too much," she said.

"What do you mean?"

"Nothing. Just that things are very different there. You've grown up in America. This is where you belong. Don't imagine that you could ever go back and live in India. You'd only be fooling yourself."

"Would there be people who might remember me?" she asked.

"Of course, the whole compound is there and Gene, that's Dr Fry," said Aunt Penny.

"Is he still there?" asked Tricia.

"Yes, he's got a few more years until retirement."

"Do you think he'd mind, if I just showed up?" asked Tricia.

"I doubt it," said Aunt Penny and Tricia noticed the twitch of disapproval on her lips.

"Does he come to America very often?" asked Tricia.

"Once every three or four years."

"Do you ever see him when he comes?" asked Tricia.

"No, he doesn't usually visit Philadelphia," said Aunt Penny.

"Maybe I should write to him. After all, he did take care of me for a year. I feel as if I should thank him in some way," said Tricia.

"Patricia, you're a grown-up girl," said Aunt Penny. "If I were you I'd let things lie. Gene was very fond of you, of course, but if you were to show up in Pipra it might bring out unpleasant memories."

"What do you mean?" said Tricia.

"Well, it was a difficult decision for him to let you go," said Aunt Penny. "I'm sure he's reconciled to it, but you never know. He might prefer it if you stayed away. Some things are best forgotten."

"What made him decide to send me here?" asked Tricia.

Aunt Penny frowned.

"I think he realized that he would never be able to care for you in the way a father should. Being a single man, it was a problem. Who'd look after you? And Pipra wasn't much of a place to raise a girl. There was nothing but the local government school. Besides, he had so many responsibilities at the hospital, there was hardly time for him to bring up a daughter on his own."

"Is that the way you felt? said Tricia.

"Yes. Of course. I won't hide the fact from you. I was against the whole idea from the start. It seemed an irresponsible sort of thing for him to do, as though he hadn't thought too far ahead."

Aunt Penny hesitated for a moment and looked away.

"Besides, I knew what it was like to raise an orphan. I had tried and failed."

48

Tricia was surprised but she said nothing.

"I've never told you about Ruth. She was a girl like yourself but she'd been sent to a home in Jhansi. I met her for the first time when she was twelve or thirteen, a bright, intelligent girl. She caught my eye because she seemed so lively, so full of possibilities. The woman who ran the orphanage was a friend of mine and I asked if I could give some money towards her education. I wanted her to study at one of the better schools in Jhansi and later go on to college. In the beginning, I had no intention of adopting her. In fact, I asked my friend to keep me out of it and all through school, Ruth never knew that I was paying. I didn't want her to feel an obligation. When she passed her high school exams, my friend and I decided that she should do her teachers' training and we sent her to Fatehgarh. By then, she'd guessed that someone was supporting her. After the first year of training, she went back to Jhansi and asked my friend to tell her who it was. There was nothing to be done. We couldn't hide it from her any longer and the next thing I knew, Ruth arrived in Pipra. She had come to thank me, but I realized that she was really searching for something else. There was nothing I could do but take her in. She was not doing well at college and took an extra year to finish the course. I hadn't seen her since she was a girl and I could tell that she had changed. Ruth was no longer the bright and cheerful student whom I'd met in Jhansi, but a sullen, moody girl. I never officially adopted her but she began to treat me as her mother. I used to get very impatient with her sometimes, because she was so dependent on me.

"After she finished her teachers' training, she wasn't able to get a job. I sent her for several interviews but everyone turned her down. I kept telling Ruth that she couldn't go on living with me forever but she didn't seem to care. Anyway, about a year after she had finished her degree, a gentleman arrived in Pipra, who's name was Mr Samson. He claimed he was a Christian and rented a room on the compound. After a couple of weeks he purchased some land nearby and built a brick kiln. Everyone was impressed with his manners and self-confidence. He seemed to bring new life into the compound. Sometimes he could be abrasive, but generally he seemed a likeable man.

"Mr Samson became quite interested in Ruth and visited our house several times on one pretext or another. To be quite honest, I was relieved to see that Ruth began to show some interest in him.

49

She was pretty enough but very shy. Don't imagine that it was a very romantic courtship. Things don't happen that way in India. In fact, I think he came to see her four or five times at the most, before asking her to marry him. She told him that he had to get my permission and he came to my office with a bouquet of Canna lilies, almost as though he was going to propose to me. I told him that it was entirely Ruth's decision and after quite a bit of back and forth, she finally agreed.

"He turned out to be a rotten egg, the worst kind of huckster that you could find. After the marriage, he moved into my bungalow, saying that he was going to build a house as soon as he got an architect. I should never have believed him. I found out later that he was heavily in debt with several money lenders in Pipra. The brick kiln was not earning as much as he had hoped. I really don't know what his true intentions were, but Ruth was very unhappy with him. It soon was obvious that he drank a lot. I would have thrown him out if it weren't for Ruth, and should have done it anyway before it was too late. Once or twice I heard him shouting at Ruth, but I kept out of it, because I didn't want to interfere.

"Then one night he woke me up and said that she was gone. It must have been two o'clock in the morning. He said that he'd been out to dinner with a friend and when he came back, she wasn't there. I'd been working late at the hospital and hadn't seen Ruth since breakfast. It seemed a peculiar thing for her to do but he insisted that she had run away with another man. I really didn't believe that it was possible and figured that he had probably shouted at her and she had got upset and left the house. She had been acting strange for awhile. There was no note to say where she was going and Mr Samson seemed so upset that nobody suspected him. I must say, I didn't like him very much, but I never thought he would be capable of murder.

"The police were more suspicious when we brought them in. They knew several things about Mr Samson already. He had been involved with some bad characters in the town.

"As we discovered later, he had come back home while I was still at the hospital and in a fit of temper – I'm sure that he was drunk – he started beating Ruth and finally killed her. Frightened of the consequences, he took her to the kiln, which had just been filled with bricks and was ready to be fired. He buried her body underneath a pile of wood, hoping that she would be consumed in the fire. His plan would have succeeded, except that some of the labourers discovered Ruth's bones when they uncovered the bricks about a week later. The police arrested him and he gave a full confession."

Aunt Penny told the story in a cold, detached manner but Tricia could sense that Ruth's death had affected her in a way that she would never admit. Sitting there in the small apartment with the rosewood elephants and the pictures of Indian monuments, Tricia could feel the distances, the lines of latitude stretching beyond the furthest horizon. India seemed so far away and yet she could hear the sound of people talking, vague and musical voices which sang in her ears, as though she'd held a conch to her ear and heard the oceans of the womb.

When Aunt Penny died in her sleep a few months later, the family made their last visit to Philadelphia. This time there was no music on the radio and no arguments, only a cold and sheath-like silence. After a short memorial service in the basement chapel, at which a missionary minister from Pakistan spoke about Aunt Penny and prayed in Urdu, his voice resonant and powerful, she was cremated at the mortuary next door. Fritz controlled himself during the service and afterwards, when the mortician presented them with the pewter urn. It was only when he tried to read her will that he broke down in tears, as though the meagre savings which his aunt had apportioned out, touched a banker's nerve and made him weep. Tricia finally had to take the paper from his hand and read aloud. Most of her money was bequeathed to the hospital in Pipra, for them to do with as they wanted. The rest was divided equally between the cousin in Nebraska, Fritz and Tricia. Each of them received about a thousand dollars. The furniture and books in her room were given over to the retirement home and the rosewood elephants went back to Hartford in the car. The only real surprise in the will, was that Aunt Penny requested her ashes should be buried in the cemetary at Pipra. This was something she had never spoken about but there it was, written down in her firmest hand, without any explanation or excuse, a simple statement of desire.

The urn was carried back to Hartford, packed in a cardboard box and carefully placed in the rear of the station wagon. It made them all uncomfortable, carrying her remains, so freshly burned.

51

When they got back home, Fritz took the urn into the guest room and placed it on the dressing table, as if it were an ornamental vase. With Aunt Penny's death Tricia felt a special sense of loss, as though her only link with India had now been severed. More than ever before, she was determined to go back and visit Pipra. She decided right then that she would take the urn herself.

SIX

TRICIA OPENED her eyes, disorientated and afraid. The mosquito netting was like a cocoon and she could see nothing beyond the fine mesh. The fan had stopped and the air was still and suffocating. Tricia vaguely remembered lying down to sleep. She had taken off her clothes because of the heat and the sheets were damp with perspiration.

It was impossible to tell the time of day in the semi-darkness of the room. The tides of her body were at their lowest ebb and she lay there like a beached fish, unable to turn herself. The heat made Tricia feel as if she were drugged. One of her arms was pinned beneath her. She withdrew it slowly and as the circulation returned there was a painful sensation, as though she'd put her hand in nettles. Closing her eyes, Tricia began to drift listlessly back into sleep, but the pins and needles in her arm seemed to get worse. Reluctantly, she wormed her way out from under the mosquito netting.

In the bathroom, she filled the enamel basin and splashed water onto her face. Tricia brushed her teeth and the flavour of the toothpaste made her feel a little wider awake. After combing her hair, she put on her clothes and found her watch. It was six o'clock. She had slept for seven hours.

The living room lay in darkness. Tricia tried the light switch several times before she remembered that the electricity was off. Fry's door was closed and there seemed to be nobody around. She was about to go back into her room, when she heard a tapping at the front door. It took her a moment to realize where the sound was coming from.

She went across to the door and opened it, pushing the thatch aside. There was a man standing on the step. He was simply dressed in trousers and shirt, with rubber chappals on his feet. His hair was cropped quite short and he had a beard. He looked a little like a tramp and there was something in his eyes that worried her, a look of fierce intensity. For a moment they stared at each other. Finally the man spoke in Hindustani.

"You want to see Dr Fry?" she said.

He nodded.

"He might be at the hospital," she said.

The man spoke once more in Hindustani, shaking his head.

"Well, let me check," she said, "I just woke up."

She started to shut the door, hesitated and then turned back to him.

"Will you come in?" she said.

He stepped past her through the door and then waited for Tricia to lead the way. There was a hostility about the man which troubled her. He seemed resentful and angry but she couldn't quite make sense of it. A little frightened, she wondered whether she had done the right thing by letting him in. Tricia motioned for him to sit down in the living room and knocked on Fry's door.

"Come in," said the reassuring voice.

She pushed open the door and stepped inside. Dr Fry was hanging from a makeshift trapeze, his feet a few inches off the ground. He grinned at her, his face red with exertion.

"I'm just stretching my back a little," said Fry, explaining. "I thought it might help." He let go of the trapeze and dropped to the ground with a grunt of pain.

"There's somebody here to see you," said Tricia, flustered.

Fry hitched up his khaki shorts and followed her into the living room.

"Hello, Gautam," he said, with surprise. The two men shook hands. Both of them seemed on guard, cautious towards each other.

"Have you met?" asked Fry, turning to Tricia.

"We haven't actually been introduced," said Tricia.

"Gautam, I'd like you to meet Patricia, my . . . " Fry hesitated. "What shall I call you? My godchild . . . Tricia, this is Gautam."

Tricia smiled weakly at the man and stretched out her hand. To her surprise, he folded his palms instead. She was confused and withdrew her hand, not knowing how to respond. Gautam stared at her with a sharp, inquisitive expression of distrust. Fry had spoken to him in English, but so far he had said nothing in return. There was an incongruity about him that puzzled Tricia, the torn and wrinkled clothes, the ascetic appearance and the look of suppressed anger in his eyes. She could tell that he was educated and yet by all appearances he seemed to live in poverty.

Ghulam Rusool appeared from the direction of the kitchen.

"How about some coffee?" said Fry, attempting to ease the tension.

"Yes, please," said Tricia. She felt she needed it.

Gautam shook his head and asked for a glass of water. He spoke in Hindustani.

Tricia wondered whether she had offended him in some way. It wasn't just unfriendliness. There was an accusation in his stare.

After a few moments, Gautam consciously averted his eyes. He began to speak with Fry. His voice sounded coarse and questioning. Tricia couldn't help but listen, even though she didn't understand a word. Dr Fry was also speaking in Hindustani and they seemed to be discussing some sort of plans.

When the glass of water arrived, Gautam took it from the cook and tilted his head back. He drank without touching the rim of the glass to his mouth. The water went down his throat in one long swallow. Fry looked at Tricia and smiled.

"We have a clinic each week in the nearby villages," he said, trying to explain, "for those who can't make it all the way to the hospital. It's held in a different place each time. I was telling Gautam we're going out on Saturday to Kaproli, which is about ten miles from here. You might like to come along. It's a beautiful spot, in the middle of the forest."

Gautam put down his glass and wiped his beard with the back of his hand. Then almost impatiently, he got to his feet. He seemed unwilling to accept Fry's hospitality. Ignoring Tricia, Gautam started to leave.

Fry got up and led him to the door.

Tricia watched him go with a feeling of apprehension, unsettled by the abrupt encounter and unable to understand this man. He seemed agitated, on the point of losing his temper.

Fry came back, shaking his head.

"Did I say something wrong?" asked Tricia.

"Don't mind Gautam," he said, "he's a little hot-headed but he's a good man underneath."

"I felt as though I had offended him," said Tricia.

Fry laughed. "That's the way he is with everybody. Gautam always looks as though he's going to chew your head off."

Ghulam Rusool arrived with two cups of coffee. At the same moment the electricity came back on, the bare bulbs splashing the room with yellow light and the fans spinning back to life.

"Did you have a good sleep?" asked Fry.

"Yes," said Tricia, "like someone knocked me out. When I woke up I didn't know where I was."

The two of them stirred their coffee in silence.

"What does he do?" she asked.

"You mean, Gautam?" said Fry, glancing up at her. "He's a social worker."

"For the hospital?" said Tricia.

"Yes," said Fry. "His father is the pastor of the church."

"He doesn't look like a social worker," said Tricia.

"Actually, he's very good at his job and spends most of his time in the villages, working with the tribals."

"Doesn't he speak English?" said Tricia.

"Oh he does," said Fry. "But he doesn't like to use it. Gautam actually did three years of college in Delhi."

By the way Fry spoke, Tricia could tell that he was fond of Gautam, in a tolerant sort of way.

"When he came back to Pipra, after college, he was very bitter and rebellious. He had changed his name from Gideon to Gautam and made a point of telling everyone that he was no longer a Christian. When Gautam came to me and asked for a job, I knew he'd never fit in at the hospital but I figured he'd be a good social worker in the villages. Of course, everyone on the compound was against me hiring him."

"Why?" said Tricia. "I don't understand."

"Well, it was partly because he'd given up being a Christian. They felt he had betrayed his community. He was very obvious about it too and got a lot of people quite disturbed. His parents had virtually disowned him. After living with them for a month or two, he moved off the compound and got a room in town. It was quite an awkward situation. People said he had become a communist. That didn't go down very well. There are a lot of people on the compound who still think I should get rid of him."

"Why haven't you?" said Tricia.

"Because he's so good at his work, so committed. The villagers like him very much. He has a way with them, a real rapport."

"It doesn't bother you that he's not a Christian?" said Tricia.

Dr Fry thought a moment.

"No," he said. "No, it doesn't. That's the funny thing. In some ways I think he's more of a Christian than a lot of people on this compound. He may not believe in God but whatever it is that he does believe in, I admire his dedication. I've never known anybody who worked as hard as him. He spends most of his time out in the villages, checking on patients, making sure they're taking the correct medicines, helping to mediate disputes, filling out government forms for those who cannot write, helping to process papers through the district offices, and basically just listening to the problems people have and trying to help them come up with positive solutions.

"I guess he's what you call an activist. Two years ago there was some trouble in this area. A lot of illegal felling was going on in the forest. The tribal people were getting upset. Gautam got involved in an agitation to stop some timber contractors from carrying away the trees. He led all kinds of strikes and demonstrations, black flags, slogans, that sort of thing. It turned nasty after a while. Like I said, he's headstrong and when he believes in something, nothing can come in his way."

Fry sipped his coffee slowly.

"There was some violence. One of the lumber trucks got burned. The accusations started going back and forth. The contractors were powerful men, with plenty of political clout. They brought in their thugs and roughed up a couple of villagers. Gautam was getting petitions ready and sending them to Delhi, writing all kinds of articles in the papers. You wouldn't expect this kind of trouble in a small place like Pipra but people were getting angry. At some point Gautam was arrested. We had to put up bail for him but as soon as we did he was out again, raising Cain. Finally the contractors sent their thugs after him. They beat him up pretty badly, broke both his legs and his jaw; left him for dead and he would have died if some of the villagers hadn't found him and brought him to the hospital. He was conscious but covered with blood. He couldn't talk because of his jaw. A lot of people told me afterwards that we shouldn't have got involved, but I didn't have much choice. He was in bad shape for about a month, a terrible patient. A lot of people wanted me to fire Gautam and said that he was giving the hospital a bad name but in a way I couldn't help sympathizing with what he was doing, even though I didn't agree with his methods. Anyway, he was laid up for a couple of months and things cooled down. The only problem with Gautam is that he can't control his temper."

"I suppose there's a lot to be angry about," said Tricia.

"What do you mean?"

"The poverty," she said. "I don't know how you deal with it."

Fry smiled to himself.

"I guess a person just gets hardened." he said.

"No, it must be different for you. You're always helping other people, giving them medicines, curing their diseases. But for me . . . it makes me feel so hopeless."

Fry looked at her and winked. He put down the cup of coffee and slowly cracked his knuckles one by one.

"There's only so much anyone can do," he said.

Tricia wondered what he really felt. She knew that he was not the kind of man who spoke his mind. But Dr Fry's cheerfulness and optimism made no sense to her, how anyone could face disease and suffering with such complacency.

SEVEN

Tricia picked up a handful of earth and let it fall into the grave. There was a dull, rattling sound as the small pebbles landed on the pewter urn. One by one the others did the same, stepping forward and tossing a handful of soil into the narrow hole. Almost all of the compound was present, about thirty to forty people altogether. Padre Massey led the service, wearing his white cassock and scarlet stole. He spoke quietly and with a sombre dignity that reminded Tricia of Gautam's manner. There were similarities between father and son. Gautam did not attend the burial, though Tricia half-expected him to be there. The cemetery seemed less stark and barren with all of the mourners gathered under the eucalyptus tree and since the service was in the evening, the sun was not so harsh. Padre Massey spoke in Hindustani, using a phrase or two of English from time to time. A few of the women wept but it seemed they did it more from habit than any genuine sadness. There were a few bouquets of flowers covered with yellow cellophane. The vine on the kikad tree appeared more brilliant than before and gave a festive look to the cemetery.

Dr Fry was wearing a rumpled suit which fit him loosely. He looked stern and self-conscious, so much taller than everyone else. Tricia stood beside him and stared at the mound of reddish earth. The grave looked like the burrow of some giant mole.

Tricia couldn't help but feel a strange detachment from the ceremony, even though she was the only "family" member there. Somehow, they were not burying Aunt Penny, the old woman in the retirement home, but a different person, Miss Reynolds, the nursing superintendent from Pipra. For Tricia, these were two different women and it was only when Padre Massey began to pray that she could hear echoes of the missionary minister in Philadelphia, his resonant Urdu, calling upon God in a foreign tongue. Only then did the two services come together and she felt as though her aunt was finally being put into the ground.

They left the cemetery in silence, dividing into smaller groups, as two of the malis from the hospital filled the rest of the earth into the grave. A truck went by on the road as they headed back towards the compound, the driver leaning out of the window to get a closer look at this strange procession. Each person had offered Tricia their condolences and Padre Massey held her hand for a long time, as if to comfort her, but she could tell they were uncertain whether Tricia should be treated as family or not.

"It was a nice service," said Dr Fry, putting a hand on her shoulder. "Padre Massey said a lot of good things about your aunt."

"Were they true?" she asked, looking at him with open eyes.

Fry smiled at her and shrugged.

"Of course," he said.

"People ususaly say so many things they don't mean at funerals. Once you're dead, everything is forgiven," said Tricia.

"Your aunt did a great deal for the church and the hospital here in Pipra," Fry said.

Tricia wondered what it would have been like if Fry had really adopted her and tried to imagine herself growing up under the constant gaze of those sad, paternal eyes. Maybe if she had been with him since childhood, she might have felt differently towards him. He would have been a good father, she thought, kind and indulgent, a little absent-minded. She wondered what it would have been like to sit with him at breakfast every morning. As she grew up, Tricia might have even kept house for him, made his bed in the mornings, chosen different curtains, made the bungalow a brighter place, put flowers in all the rooms. She would have been a good daughter to him, protective and considerate.

When Tricia and Dr Fry got back to the house, they found that the electricity was off again. Because the house was so dark they decided to sit in the angan. Fry went inside and brought out a piece of wood which he was carving into the shape of a leg. It was for one of the patients, a villager who'd lost his leg in an accident. Fry had ordered an artificial limb from Delhi but when it arrived it was for the left leg instead of the right and he had decided that he could do a better job of it himself.

Tricia said, "Sometimes I feel like one of those people that have their arms or legs amputated and afterwards when it's healed and there's only a stump, they get this feeling like it's still there and they can actually touch things with it."

"Phantom limbs," said Dr Fry.

"It's as though the severed nerves keep sending signals to my brain," she said.

"What do you mean?" said Fry.

"I don't remember anything of Pipra," she said, "but there's a kind of emptiness where the memories should have been."

He smiled and she could tell that he wasn't taking her seriously. Dr Fry didn't have much time for introspection.

"When I was a kid," said Tricia, "I used to think that I had lived in India a long time ago, in another incarnation. I used to imagine that I had been a princess, surrounded by jewels and peacock feathers. I'd make up all kinds of crazy stories about myself when I was young."

"You're still young," he said, playfully.

"Do you believe in reincarnation?" she asked.

He shook his head.

"I figure, one life's enough," he said.

There was a stunted custard apple tree in the courtyard and a purple bougainvillea against the wall. Fry kept carving as they talked. The wood was a reddish colour, light-weight but very strong. Fry worked slowly, patiently, using the jack-knife which Tricia had given him.

"When are you going to go back to America?" she asked.

"I don't know," he said. "I'm due for a furlough, but the problem is I'm going to be sixty-five next year, which means I'm ready to retire."

"You don't have to, do you?" she said.

"The mission has its rules," he said, making an oblique gesture with his hand. "They've been sending me fliers and pamphlets for the last few years, the Presbyterian pension fund, Golden Acres retirement home, Elysium Pastures. I guess it's all supposed to make you feel secure, but it gives me the creeps."

"I can't imagine this place without you," said Tricia. "The hospital would probably fall apart."

"I don't think so," he said, without looking up from his carving.

She was the first person he had spoken to about leaving Pipra. He had gone over it in his mind at least a hundred times, trying to decide what he should do, but thinking about retirement always made him feel uneasy.

"What would you do if you retired?" she asked.

"I've always thought of buying a camper and travelling around America. There are a lot of places I haven't seen, like the Grand Canyon."

"All by yourself?" she said.

He looked up at her with as though the question hadn't meant anything to him.

"You can always come and live with me," said Tricia, half-teasing.

"What would you do when your friends came around? Put me in a rocking chair on the back porch?" he asked. There was no malice in his words. He meant it as a joke.

"I don't have those kind of friends," she said. "No wild parties."

"Aren't you going to get married some day?" he asked.

"No thanks," she said, clowning for him.

Tricia felt a brief, nostalgic sense of home; Hartford, a summer evening. She could hear the good-humour man ringing his bell. She could feel the heat radiating off the sidewalk, the smell of cedar needles underfoot, the blackflies, the monotonous feeling of summer days.

"You love this country, don't you?" said Tricia.

"I guess so."

"No, I mean, really," she said. "I can't imagine you in the States. This is where you belong."

He grinned at her with a sidelong glance. The leg was nearly finished; he needed to do a little more on the ankle and the heel, then sand it down.

"I always enjoy going back to America," he said. "For the first week I'm there, I don't do anything except eat ice cream and watch TV."

"I don't believe you," said Tricia, making a face.

"The other thing I like to do is to go to hardware stores," said Fry. "One of those places where you can get everything from a monkey wrench to a tube of rubber cement."

"What do you watch on TV?" asked Tricia.

"I like baseball. That's the only thing I really miss, not knowing what's happening in the world series. Last time I made sure I was there for the whole season, watched every game. I didn't know any of the player's names, even the teams had changed, different cities, different pennants."

"I don't think there's anything more boring than baseball," said Tricia.

"That's because you don't understand the game," he said. "Nothing like it, bases loaded, bottom of the ninth, Mantle swats a line drive and they're home. Football can't compare. I used to play in college – short stop."

Tricia smiled as she watched him carving against the grain of the wood, careful that he didn't cut too deep.

"Are there any other missionaries around?" she asked.

He thought a moment.

"Three of them at the Seminary in Jagatpur," he said, "that's about four hours from here. We get together at Christmas time. It's not like it used to be. There were six of us in Pipra."

"How long ago was that?" she asked.

"Fifty-eight, fifty-nine," he said. "After that, people started to leave. The last person to go was Miss Reynolds. She retired in sixty-eight."

"You've been alone since then?" she asked.

"Not exactly," he said, with a crooked smile.

"Don't you ever get depressed?" she asked.

"Sure," he said. "All the time."

"What keeps you going?"

"The work, I suppose," said Fry. "More than anything, just knowing that there are people over there in the hospital who need my skills. There's always another patient. I just can't stop, that's all."

"Don't you ever feel like giving up?" she said.

"Sometimes," he said, "when I think I'm getting old."

"And lonely?" said Tricia.

He shook his head, staring down at the wood chips on the ground.

"There's hardly time for that," he said.

"Do you ever take vacations?" she asked.

"Only when I go back to the States; in front of the TV," he said.

Just then, the blade of the knife slipped and he sliced his finger.

"Ouch," said Tricia.

Fry put the finger to his mouth and sucked on it. After a few moments, he looked at it, the blood seeping out from under the flap of skin.

"It's not very deep," he said.

"Can I get you something to put on it?" asked Tricia.

"There must be some band-aids on my dressing table," said Fry.

She went inside to his bedroom. The electricity was still not on and the bungalow was like an oven. Her eyes adjusted slowly to the gloom. The dressing table stood against one wall and was cluttered with different objects. While Tricia was searching for the bandaids, she came upon a picture in a metal frame. It was a black and white photograph of a woman with short blonde hair. She was pretty in an old-fashioned sort of way, a cheerful, sunburnt face and sharp, pale eyes. Slowly, Tricia put the picture back on the dressing table and found the bandaids. When she went outside, Fry was carving again, sucking at his finger between each slice of the blade.

"Thanks, Patricia," he said, taking the box from her and choosing one. "You know there's a church in New Jersey which keeps us supplied with bandaids. They send us about five thousand every year."

As Tricia helped him put the bandaid on his finger, she touched the gold wedding band on his left hand.

"You were married once?" she asked.

Fry looked up at her with surprise.

"Yes, I was," he said.

"I saw her picture on the dressing table . . . " said Tricia.

His eyes moved from her face to his hands. He closed the blade of the knife with a snap.

"What happened?" she said.

"My wife was killed the year after we were married." He said, without looking up. Tricia sat down slowly on the step beside him.

"We came to India in 1941," said Fry. "The war was going on. I was just out of medical school. They wouldn't take me in the army because I had a trick knee which used to go out all the time in those days. My wife had always wanted to be a missionary and I was interested in seeing some other part of the world, besides Ohio. We had been together in high-school in a little town called Irving. We applied to the board of foreign missions. They needed doctors in India and my wife had done a course in seminary. We were both twenty-six. As soon as we got to Bombay, we heard that the Japanese were invading Burma. It looked as though India was next. Anyway, we got a train to Pipra, which was about as far away from the war as you could get. But things were starting to get scary. The board of foreign missions sent a letter around, about four or five months after we arrived, suggesting that women and children should be sent back to America. My wife had just decided that she was pregnant. We didn't know what to do. Everybody else was packing up. She didn't want to leave and I was all confused. Finally

64

they convinced me, the others, that I should send her back. It was pretty awful. We went to Bombay. Everything was very tense. The American consulate put her on the list and told us that they'd give us twenty-four hours notice. You see, they couldn't give out any details about the ships that were coming and going. Mostly they were liners converted into troopships with a few cabins reserved for civilian passengers. There were submarines outside the port. We got a room at the mission guest house and waited. We didn't know when she would leave. It could have been the next morning or a month from then. We didn't know when we were going to see each other again. Anyway, her turn finally came. I took her down to the docks but they wouldn't allow me beyond a certain point. They wouldn't even tell me the name of the ship – tight security, hundreds of soldiers all around. We didn't know where the ship was taking her, whether it would sail to San Diego or New York. We didn't know how long it would take. That same night, after I put her on the ship, I caught the train back to Pipra. I kept feeling I'd made a mistake. The Japanese would never invade. Once you got out of Bombay the war was only on the radio.

"She hadn't gone on the same ship as the other women from Pipra, something about alphabetical order. They'd split them up, A to L and M to Z. There were some others staying at the guest house who went with her, an old couple from the Punjab who were retiring. I had an anxious feeling. I don't usually believe in premonitions, but it could have been this time, this once . . .

"About a month after I got back to Pipra, word came that her ship had been sunk by a Japanese destroyer, somewhere near Sumatra. She wasn't one of the survivors. They'd been torpedoed. We didn't get many details because it was all very sensitive at the time. The worst of it was, I got a letter from her afterwards. Their ship had docked in Colombo. Someone was getting off and she had given them a letter to mail. It had a censor's stamp on it and looked as though it had travelled around in someone's pocket for some time. This was about two months after I'd heard she died – I thought they'd found her. She was alive. But as I started to read the letter, I realized it had been written before. She said that she was seasick all the way from Bombay and with the baby coming it was worse."

He hadn't told anyone the story for more than twenty years and Tricia was the first person to know about the letter. Fry could feel a lingering sadness. He could hear it in his own voice, but it was very far away.

"What was she like?" asked Tricia, trying to make the picture on the dressing table come to life.

"She was pretty," said Fry, "and deeply religious. Like I said, she was the one who really wanted to become a missionary. I don't think I would have come to India, if it hadn't been for her. She was a lovely person, spoke softly, never angry . . . except maybe once, when I decided to take up smoking a pipe. That was the only time she scolded me." He laughed as though the recollection had struck him unaware.

"What was her name?" asked Tricia.

Fry's expression was a mixture of guilt and mischief.

"It was Patricia," he said.

She stared at him.

"I'm sorry," he said. "I wasn't going to tell you."

"It's okay," she said, trying to make it seem as if it didn't matter for his sake.

"We had to give you a name," said Fry, apologetic. "Your mother never gave you one."

"Somehow I thought Fritz and Sally had been the ones who named me. Sally had a favourite Aunt Patricia."

Fry stared at the wooden leg with a blank expression on his face as if he had suddenly discovered that it was there. Tricia stood up and went across to him, took his face in her hands and kissed him. He tried to kiss her back but he was awkward and made a smacking noise in the air next to her cheek. His hands smelled of disinfectant. He was crying now, the tears running down the creases of his face. Tricia let herself be drawn into his arms and wept on his shoulder, feeling the unknowable past converge on her like the suction of a terrible vacuum. She could feel the torpedo entering the hull of the ship and the floor of the cabin listing slowly, could feel the shudder of the engines and hear the sirens and the cries, the waves slapping over the portholes, the stars disappearing in the foam, the sound of rushing water . . .

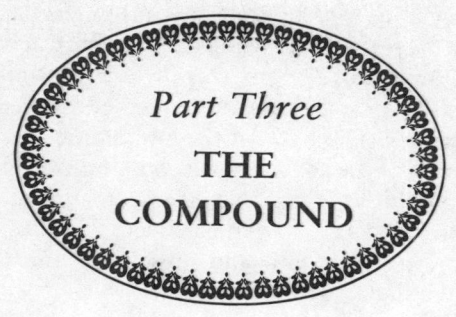

Part Three

THE COMPOUND

ONE

BEING SATURDAY, our teacher let us out at noon, after we had finished our maths. Jojeph, Sunil and I were walking home together, carrying slates and satchels. The days were getting warmer, the sort of weather in which our mothers forced us to wear pullovers and we took them off as soon as we were out of the compound gate. Another month and school would close for the summer. There was feeling of brightness and change in the air, as if the sky was shedding its skin like a snake.

Beyond the octroi barrier, a road gang was repairing one of the culverts which had collapsed during last year's monsoon. There was a barricade of empty oil drums and a detour off to the left; a rutted, dusty track which crossed the drainage ditch and circled up the other side. We stopped and watched the men breaking stones and carrying baskets of dirt on their heads. It would be another month or two before they finished, just in time for the next monsoon to wash it all away again. The PWD contractor stood with his hands clasped behind his chequered coat, telling us to move along because he knew, first chance we got, one of us would write our name in the wet cement.

Just then we saw the hospital ambulance turning out of the compound gate. As it came closer we could see that Dr Fry was behind the wheel. He was wearing dark glasses and didn't look in our direction. Beside him in the front seat was Miss Reynolds, the nursing superintendent. I hardly recognized her out of the uniform, without the starched white hat pinned to her hair. They slowed down before the detour and rolled up their windows because of the

dust. Miss Reynolds was holding the girl in her lap. They were
going to catch the train to Delhi and from there an aeroplane would
take them to America. The girl was dressed in a pink frock and
waving to nobody in particular. She seemed excited and happy,
ribbons in her hair. The back of the ambulance was loaded with
suitcases and two of the hospital sweepers who were going along to
carry Miss Reynolds's luggage. Next thing, the ambulance plunged
down the detour and a cloud of dust covered us all: the road gang,
the contractor, Jojeph, Sunil and myself. By the time the dust
settled, the ambulance was out of sight.

"When will she reach America?" said Jojeph. "Before tonight?"

"No. They will only get to Delhi tomorrow morning," said Sunil.

"Besides, it's night in America when it's daytime here," I said,
remembering what my father had told me.

The whole compound had turned out to see Miss Reynolds off and
as we came down the driveway past the church, I could see them
standing in front of her bungalow, talking amongst themselves. A
group of nurses were headed back towards the hospital, speaking in
high, excited voices. They were probably glad to see Miss Reynolds
go, the way she scolds and bosses them.

Everyone was standing around in the sun, glad for an excuse to
be out of doors. Father was talking with one of the junior doctors
and Mr Ezekiel from accounts. It looked as though church had just
let out, except that father wasn't wearing his cassock. They ignored
us as we came along. Mother and the other women were knotted
together near the peepul tree, whispering as always. I knew that
they were talking about Mamta and what had happened, how she
had run away and left the child. Thinking of Mamta, I wanted to go
and hide near the castor trees at the far corner of the compound,
where we used to pretend that we were in the jungle and Mamta
would sit with us and tell us stories about the real forests beyond
the mountains, but Jojeph had already run ahead to his mother and
Sunil and I were being called.

"You should have hurried, Gideon," said my mother. "Now
they've gone."

"We saw them," said Sunil. "They passed us on the road."

"Maybe they'll miss the train. It's already time."

"No. The Delhi train is always late," said mother.

I secretly hoped that they would miss the train. Up until I saw them drive away, I hadn't thought about her leaving. To me the most important thing had been that they were going in an aeroplane. I saw one long ago, flying overhead like a silver insect, way above us. The purring of its motors filled the sky. I remember telling Mamta what it was and she refused to believe me, saying nothing could go that high, even though she saw it for herself. There was a strange look in her eyes as she stared at the aeroplane, a kind of emptiness, as though the plane was already carrying the girl away.

Miss Reynolds would be back after a year's furlough, but the girl would stay in America forever. She was being adopted by Miss Reynolds's nephew and his wife. The way they talked, my mother and the other Christian women, I could tell that they were jealous, how this girl, hardly a year old, could be sent away to America. It is their way of thinking, really, that one of us deserved to go much more than the daughter of some tribal girl. I think that my mother would have gladly sent me off to be adopted by Americans, if she'd had the chance.

That afternoon they were sitting in the sun, warming themselves after their baths, hair loose and oiled about their shoulders; Binu's mother and Jojeph's and old Mrs Samuel who is going bald, talking like mynas in a palm tree, shaking their heads in disappointment. Old Mrs Samuel has a cousin in America, in Chicago, where he runs a shop or something, and he sends her gifts from there. She claims he makes twenty thousand rupees a month and wants to buy some land in Pipra and build a house; not just yet, but in a year or two.

"Lies," says mother, "he probably works as a street cleaner since his people are sweeper-christians."

Mrs Samuel is deaf and the other women will sit and talk about her as if she wasn't there. But today they are mostly interested in the girl and what will become of her in America.

"So small, so dark," says mother. "They'll probably think she's a hubshee from Africa."

People were surprised enough when Dr Fry kept the girl and wondered whether he had lost his mind, a single man to bring up a daughter on his own; nobody could understand. It is better that the girl should be sent away from Pipra, somewhere it doesn't matter who she is. They should have given her to an orphanage right away and let the whole thing be forgotten. What child would ever want to know that she had been abandoned? Better that she never hear the truth about her mother, a dirty tribal girl straight out of the jungle, who knew more witchcraft than babycare. She probably lied to us and never had a husband.

"Gideon, why are you always listening?" says mother. "Such things a boy doesn't need to hear."

"They always take better care of orphans," said Binu's mother. "Our children never get the same."

But she isn't an orphan, I wanted to say.

"It's always been that way with the missionaries," said mother. "Orphans get the scholarships and schools. Look at Ruth. The Miss-sahib spoiled her like a pet."

"And see what happened."

That was four years ago, when I was younger and didn't understand these things, what it means to be an orphan. My mother is always saying how we are Christians from a long time back, as if she means our family is more pure.

"Your grandfather, my father, was Rajinder Adams, who came to Allahabad from Lahore in 1947. Your grandmother was Miriam and she was a teacher at the Women's College in Lahore where Reverend and Mrs Adams were the Principals. It was their name that my grandfather took when he converted. They were English. We were three sisters, your aunties Shushila, Reeta and I. Your grandfather had a brother and sister, Karamjit Adams and Priya Adams. She is still living in Ferozepur, where she was a nurse. The two brothers are dead and buried in Allahabad. Isaac Adams, my grandfather, who used to be a brahmin before he converted, married into the Joseph family. His wife was the youngest daughter, Rebecca Joseph, of the famous Padre Tariq Joseph of Farrukabad. She had four brothers, Abraham, Nicodemus and Edward and it is her great grandson who is engaged to be married to Mrs Samuel's grand-daughter. The Josephs of Indore are the descendants of Edward Joseph, the youngest brother. Nicodemus went to Canada and became a doctor. His grandson came out and took a wife back with him only last year, Hosanna Solomon of Madinpur. Padre Tariq Joseph married Magdalene Masih, the daughter of Padre Barkat Masih of Morena, who was famous for his preaching among the dacoits. He himself had been a dacoit. It is through him that your father and I are related. We are his great-great-grandchildren. Your father's name was changed from Masih to Massey by one of his uncles. He is descended from Sikander Masih the only son of Padre Barkat Masih. There was a third daughter who married a Muslim and was thrown out of the house by her father . . ."

We are all related, it seems. For my mother it is important to know these relationships because it gives her a feeling of security. Mother's voice seems a chant almost, an incantation. For her, Christianity is no more than a genealogy. It is not a faith, as it is with father, as it must have been with Padre Barkat Masih, whom I have heard stories about. He faced the anger of the dacoit chieftains, evangelizing amongst those violent bandits. In mother there is no belief or sincerity. It is only her family connections which matter. That is why she has no love for orphans.

TWO

BINU TOLD US what she had heard, though I didn't believe her, even if she says her father told her mother in front of her. She said that Ruth had run away with some man from Indore. They had left the night before. She told her husband she was going over to see old Mrs Samuel and the man must have been waiting. They were gone. Nobody knew him except that Mrs Samuel had seen him waiting behind her house in the shadow of a mulberry tree, though Binu's father said that this was probably a lie. The old woman had enough trouble seeing during the day, but at night she couldn't even count her own ten fingers.

Then the story came out and the adults stopped whispering and gossiping aloud. A police constable said that he had seen a man and a woman on a cycle going by the octroi barrier. Someone said they had heard a motorcycle during the night. My mother went over to visit Mr Samson. She stayed there a long time and when she came back she said that he was lying in bed crying, saying that he knew his wife would leave some time and that he had seen the man once or twice hanging around the compound, waiting for him to go out. Miss Reynolds had been trying to telephone Indore all day.

Some of the compound women came over to our house that night to talk about the scandal.

"I tell you, she'll go to hell for this," said my mother.

"The saris she wore! You'd think she was a movie actress."

"It was the Miss-sahib's fault, of course, she spoiled her since she was a child, brought her things which went to her head."

"That's what happens with these orphans. They think too highly of themselves."

Ruth had been raised in an orphanage near Jhansi. Miss Reynolds had given money for her education and Ruth had done her teachers' training at Fatehgarh. She was very pale and her hair was a reddish brown. I never heard her speak. She stayed indoors most of the time, in one of the dark rooms of Miss Reynolds's bungalow. After finishing her teachers' training she came to Pipra and began living with Miss Reynolds. We only saw her at Church, the sari draped over her head and those pale hands clutching her

Bible. She would sit beside Miss Reynolds and hardly move her lips to the hymns. I never imagined her as a teacher, how she could have taught a classroom full of noisy children. I always thought she was disturbed in her mind. Sometimes we would see her watching from the window of her room, just the pale outline of her face behind the glass, peering out at us.

The winter after Ruth came back to stay, Mr Samson arrived from Jabalpur. He bought some land beyond the jheel and because he was a Christian everybody was happy to welcome him. Mother said that he had some relatives in Agra whom she knew, but nobody was really certain. He rented a room from Mr Ezekiel and I remember how he impressed everyone with his money, putting ten rupees in the collection every Sunday. He was going to build a brick kiln on the land he'd bought and hired villagers to dig the kilns. When the smoke-stacks arrived, we all went out to have a look. They were in separate pieces and he had them bolted together on the spot. Mother admired Mr Samson very much. She used to say how good it was to see a Christian making money instead of working at a hospital or teaching college.

After several weeks, I noticed Mr Samson going to Miss Reynolds's bungalow two, three times a week and before too long we heard that he was engaged to marry Ruth. Everyone seemed pleased with the match, including Miss Reynolds. Father married them in the church and even though Mr Samson had sent out invitations, none of his people came from Agra or anywhere else to attend. He still hadn't started to build his new house so Miss Reynolds offered to let them stay in half of her bungalow. She seemed to like Mr Samson, the same as everyone else and when the brick kilns started, he gave the first six cart-loads of bricks to the hospital for a new garage that was being built.

From behind the church you can see the smoke-stacks of the kilns. They seem to come out of the ground, out of nowhere, like the leafless stalks of the frangipane cuttings which father planted in front of the church, once the leaves fell off, standing straight up without any reason for being there. In the morning during winter, the steam rises from the kilns and there is always a mist over the jheel. I squat at the edge of the compound and watch the mist evaporate. As it gets thinner, the smoke from the kilns shows up dark in the middle of the white mist and you can vaguely see the smoke-stacks. Then the sun comes out and the mist disappears. All that is left are the smoke-stacks and the black smoke. There are no trees even, just the jheel, the dusty maidan, the arhar fields and in the distance, the low outline of the town.

We are not supposed to swim in the jheel or go near the smoke-stacks but we go anyway because that is our favourite place for games.

There are three kilns and one is always working. We go to watch them making bricks from the clay of the jheel. It is a grey colour and smells of frogs. They put the mud in moulds and then stack the raw bricks out to dry. When they have enough of them, the workers carry the bricks into the kilns, which are like the foundations of a large house that has never been built. The raw bricks are stacked in rows, hundreds and hundreds of them, until there are only small passages through the kiln. It is like a maze and sometimes we play hide and seek in the kiln, though the workers yell at us, saying that some day one of us will get trapped inside and be burned to death.

When the bricks are all inside, then they pile the passages full of wood. From the top they cover the kiln with dirt so that it looks as though nothing is underneath. Then they light the fire beneath the ground and the smoke starts coming out of the chimney in black clouds.

It burns like that for almost a week. The workers have wooden shoes to walk across the surface of the kiln, which gets even hotter under your feet than sand in summer. We are never allowed to walk on top. There are holes along the sides of the kiln and they let us look inside sometimes. It is all orange and red. The bricks seem to be on fire like coals and the wood is a dark, metallic colour. You can't see the flames because it is all one huge flame and when they take the covers off the holes, there is a roaring sound. It is just like hell inside.

We bring potatoes and vegetables and the workers bury these in the dirt. In five or ten minutes they dig them out when they are cooked. The workers make tea by putting a kettle of water in the dirt. It boils, the ground is so hot.

The workers then sit and wait and make more bricks for the other two kilns while the big iron smoke-stack blows out soot and sparks.

74

After a week, one morning when I am squatting at the edge of the fields, the mist clears and the smoke has stopped. The workers uncover the bricks. They come out a dark red colour, still warm from the fire. The workers carry them in baskets on their heads and pile them on bullock-carts which take them away. Inside the kiln there is nothing left but the ash from the wood. The red bricks are taken away to build houses and walls but the kiln stays empty like the abandoned foundations of a ruined building.

Mr Samson comes every day on his motorcycle to inspect the work. He is a fat man with a smooth face and red eyes. They say he drinks a lot. When he sees us, he does not say anything for we are Christian children, but when the boys from the town come to watch the bricks being made, he shouts at them and chases them away.

The evening after my mother and the ladies had been gossiping about Ruth and how she was just another ungrateful orphan, I came home from hunting doves with Kapil. Mr Samson's motorcycle was parked in front of our angaan door. First, I went up and looked at the motorcycle. It makes a noise like a grist mill. I felt the fenders. I ran my hand over the petrol tank. It felt smooth and polished and I could see my face reflected in the chrome. I wanted to get onto the motorcycle but I was afraid that it would fall over. I touched the switches on the handlebars and the mirror. Then, without knowing what I was doing, I touched the horn and it went off like an angry goose, with a long, honking noise. I jumped away.

Mr Samson came out of the door, his face angry and purple as a brinjal. He slammed the door open so hard that the latch fell off. I thought for sure he would hit me. Then he stopped and smiled as though nothing had happened.

"Hello, Gideon," he said, quickly. "Would you like to sit on the motorcycle?"

I shook my head. The horn had scared me and I didn't trust the way he smiled. Behind him I saw my father's disapproving face.

"Gideon, come inside," he said. "Don't fool with things that don't belong to you. The motorcycle might have fallen on the top of you. Then what?"

"Never mind, never mind," said Mr Samson, patting my head. He had never spoken to me before.

Mother hurried me into the kitchen and gave me milk. Together we squatted and listened to father and Mr Samson talking in the angan. They were sitting on the charpai and their voices came through the window clearly.

"Padre Massey, what can I do?" said Mr Samson. "She was always a wicked woman. Reynolds Miss-sahib was blind to her sinfulness. Everyone thought that she was quiet and homely. Even I was deceived before I married her, but inside she was evil."

"Did you think she would ever leave you?" asked my father.

"No, Padre Sahib. I guessed that there was some man whom she was seeing. But I never saw him. It is terrible, the gossip."

"In the Bible, Jesu Masih condemned gossip. You should not let your ears open to it. There is no weight to any of it. It is the chatter of the devil."

My mother smiled to herself. I know that she does not believe anything my father says. She sits in church and sings the hymns, but I know that inside of her she is laughing at father. He is very honest, though, I know that he believes what he says. People come to him and he always listens to them, though mother snickers to herself, as if she was embarrassed or scared of the truth.

"Since the beginning, Padre Massey, she was like this. After we were married, she cried and asked me to take her away from Pipra. She said there was no life there. She wanted to go to the pictures and when I told her that I never to go the pictures because you have forbidden it, she laughed at me."

I know that Mr Samson goes to pictures. I have seen him there. Once we went to the "Delite" not to see the picture but just to look at the posters and the stills in the windows, the fighting scenes and the scenes of men and women holding hands. The film let out while we were there. Hundreds of men came out of the hall and Mr Samson was among them with two or three others from the town. He was laughing and chewing a paan. Father must have known that Mr Samson was lying. He knows that most of the compound goes to the cinema hall even though he preaches against it.

"I did not know what to do with her," said Mr Samson," and the Miss-sahib was of no help at all. Anything that Ruth would say, she would agree. I was always polite and respectful. I could not raise my voice against her, otherwise Miss Reynolds would say that I was being cruel."

"God will look after her wherever she is," said father, softly.

Mother snickered again and I wanted to run outside, out to the brick kiln and watch the workers making bricks, see the kettles of tea boil in the dirt. I wanted to run away from the house and the kitchen which is always stuffy with the smell of oil and spices. But father and Mr Samson went on talking until it was dark.

Our school had been on holidays for almost a month. Every day we would collect under the gul mohur tree in the centre of the compound and decide where to go. Because she is the eldest, Binu usually decided but sometimes she would take the girls off to do one thing and I would decide what the boys should do. There was only a week of holidays left and that morning I had noticed the smoke had stopped coming from the brick kiln. Binu and the girls wanted to stay under the gul mohur tree and play their hopscotch. So I took the boys and went off through the arhar fields to the kiln and watched the workers uncovering the bricks. They had already taken most of the dirt off the top.

Mr Samson was there with his motorcycle, watching the men carrying the baskets full of dirt away and dumping them. We were standing nearby. The heat was rising from the bricks and we could feel it on our faces. Just then I heard someone shout. Two of the workmen were standing inside the kiln and one of them was holding something in his hands. All of us went closer to have a look, but before we knew what was happening, I saw Mr Samson coming after us. He looked very angry.

We took off, running into the arhar fields where we hid and watched. I couldn't understand why Mr Samson had chased us away, after he had been so friendly when I pressed the horn of his motorcycle. He chased us away the same as he chased the boys from the town away, even though we were from the church compound.

We saw him turn back to the kiln and walk to the spot where the workers were standing. All of them had gathered around. Mr Samson shouted at them, waving them aside. We were crouched in the field.

"What was it?"

"It looked like a bone," I said.

"Maybe it was a dog's bone."

"Maybe it crawled in there and they buried it alive."

"No, they would have found it."

"But are you sure it wasn't just a stick?"

"No," I said, "it was a bone, a joint, round like a table tennis ball."

"It could have been a dog that died after it crawled inside."

"Let's go back home."

"You're scared," I said. "You just want to play girl's games."

"No, I'm not scared. I just want to go back."

"Yes, I want to go back home."

"You're scared."

But I was scared as well. All I could think of was Mr Samson slamming the door open and coming at me. This time he did not smile and pat my head. He swore at me. I remembered seeing him that night, coming out of the picture hall with his arm around one of the town men, grinning and showing the red of his mouth. His mouth was all red when he grinned that night and he was laughing because he was drunk. It made me even more scared to think about him. We decided to go home, through the arhar fields, running crouched down so that Mr Samson wouldn't see us.

The police came to visit my father. The Daroga knew him and they sat together on the charpai in the angan. This time, mother put me in the bedroom from where I could hear nothing.

We were told strictly not to go to the kilns any more. From across the jheel we could see the police in their khaki uniforms, moving about under the giant chimneys. The workers were all gone. Mr Samson was also gone. They said he tried to run away but the police caught him in Madinpur as he was getting onto a bus. We never saw him again.

The next day, Miss Reynolds and my mother and some of the other women went to the kiln and they collected the bits of bones and ashes in a brass pot. There was hardly anything left. In the evening, all of us went to the graveyard, which is down the road at the far corner of the compound. Old Mr Samuel is buried there and others whom I never knew. There are some missionaries as well, their names chiselled onto the marble slabs. My father led the service and we stood around the grave with our heads bowed, the women on one side and the men on the other. Miss Reynolds was there in her white uniform and though she was not crying, I could see her hands trembling. Mother was beside me, the sari drawn over her head. Father did not mention Mr Samson or anything about the police. His voice was solemn and softer out of doors, without the echoes of the church.

"...ashes to ashes, dust to dust."

I thought of the ash which is left over after the bricks have been taken out, powdery and white. Then I remembered looking into the kiln and seeing the bones. I imagined Ruth running through the kiln as we used to do, playing hide and seek. It was all orange. It was hell and she was running around and around through the flames, screaming. The fire roared behind her.

THREE

I NEVER LIKED Miss Reynolds. She had been at the hospital since before I was born, almost as long as Dr Fry. I remember hearing my mother and the other women telling about her habits. She could never keep a servant for more than a month, before he quit because of her nagging. Either that, or she would throw him out for smoking in the kitchen or not boiling the drinking water. She was very strict and at the hospital everyone was terrified of her. One day she happened to see us buying gol-gappas from the chat-walla who pushes his cart along the road. Miss Reynolds flew at us and made us throw away the rest. She said that we would die of cholera.

She never wore anything but her starched white uniform with the little cap, like a paper boat, on her head. Even to church she would wear the same spotless dress and white stockings which made her look like a sugar goddess. I remember that Miss Reynolds would sit in the front row and sing the hymns in a shrill, warbling voice; she was the only person louder than the harmonium. One time, my father was preaching about communism and how bad it was in China and people weren't allowed to worship and the missionaries had all been killed. Somehow, he got confused and began to tell us that Chiang Kai-Shek had murdered all the Christians in Peking. He kept on saying that God would punish Chiang Kai-Shek until finally Miss Reynolds couldn't bear it any more and said in her loud voice, "Padre Massey, it's Mao Tse-Tung not Chiang Kai-Shek." For a moment, father looked at her with a worried expression and then he nodded slowly and finished his sermon with a prayer.

Each year before Christmas, Miss Reynolds would have a party for the compound children. She organized it carefully and every year it was the same. As soon as we arrived, dressed in our Sunday clothes, hair oiled and combed behind our ears; she would make us sit in rows, boys to one side, girls to other and make us sing carols in Hindustani. She had coir matting on the floor of her living room which was rough and uncomfortable to sit upon. In one corner of the room there would be a Christmas tree, decorated with coloured balls and tinsel. Underneath lay the packages for each of us. Miss Reynolds would give us cups of lemon squash and paper plates of sweets, the same thing every year. She would put on her gramophone and play a record of Christmas music in which the women always sounded like angels. Afterwards, when we had finished our squash and sweets, she would call out our names and we would go forward to collect our presents. For the boys they would be wrapped in green paper and red for the girls, always the same gift for everyone. One year the girls got knitting needles and the boys got pencil boxes; another time it was hair ribbons and geometry sets. We would say, "Thank you" politely and hurry outside and rip the paper open, imagining that this year she might just give in and buy guns with plastic bullets or something other than pencil boxes and geometry sets.

Some people said that after Ruth got burned in the brick kiln, Miss Reynolds went a little crazy. But I think that she was always that way and maybe it just made things worse. I got the feeling that Miss Reynolds hated Pipra. There was a constant look of displeasure on her face and she was always losing her temper at the nurses and the hospital sweepers, because they hadn't washed their hands or else she'd found cockroach in the general ward. As children, we lived in fear of her. Once, she caught a villager urinating against the wall of the hospital compound and marched straight up to him and shouted until he stopped. If anyone else had done it, people would have laughed but with Miss Reynolds it was a different thing completely. She knew the blood type of every person on the compound and whenever there was an emergency and they needed blood, you could be sure that she would send a chit around, asking people to come across. Everyone obeyed, even my father, who has a special kind of blood which is difficult to match.

In our games, we would often pretend that we were doctors and nurses and make a hospital of our own near the papita trees behind the church. Binu would always play Miss Reynolds. She would smear the sticky milk from the papita trees on our wounds and make bandages out of the leaves. As tablets, she gave us bits of marigold blossoms which had a medicinal taste. It was not our favourite game, but Binu insisted and she would sit there for hours pretending that we were dying from typhoid or pneumonia. Those were the diseases which she could cure. When Binu was not looking, we would try to escape into the oleander bushes, but she was quick and fierce as Miss Reynolds, making us suffer imaginary fevers and pains, taking our temperature with a neem twig. Her physical examinations were always the worst, especially for boys, and she would love to unbutton our shirts and put her ear to our chests and other things which made us get up and run away, like the time she tried to give poor Jojeph an enema.

Once, when Binu had us there, Dr Fry came past. He stopped and asked what we were playing and when we told him, "hospital", he laughed out loud. Dr Fry was very different to Miss Reynolds. He was younger, even though he'd been at the hospital much longer than Miss Reynolds. I always liked Dr Fry. He was the biggest man I'd ever seen. One time there was a circus in Pipra and this strong man came into the ring and picked up a thousand pounds with one hand. Afterwards, he challenged anyone in the crowd to a wrestling match, but everyone was too afraid. People said that the only person who might have beat him was Dr Fry. They said it as a joke because Dr Fry was not the kind of man who'd fight and I was never scared of him, despite his size. He never got angry with anyone, though I'd seen him once, repairing the hospital gate. He picked the whole thing off its hinges and straightened the iron bars with his bare hands.

He would come to our house for dinner once in a while and I would be called out to say goodnight. He would put his hand on my shoulder and ask me if I was still playing "hospital". It was something he never forgot. Dr Fry spoke softly and usually in Hindustani, not the way Miss Reynolds' speaks, as if she's talking to a servant, but properly as though it were his own language.

Dr Fry was always making something, either at the hospital or on the compound and I used to imagine him in the operating theatre with a hammer and nails, cutting people open and putting them back together again. Once he even tried to show the sweepers the kind of brooms they have in America, with a long handle, so you don't have to squat down. There he was in front of the hospital demonstrating the broom, dust and leaves flying everywhere and all of the villagers and hospital people laughing to see the sahib showing sweepers how to do their work. That was one of his inventions which never got used because the sweepers preferred their jharoos, squatting on their haunches.

One winter, we saw him doing something just outside the bungalow, in the yard to the kitchen. He had a lot of old pipes that he was fitting together with the help of one of the hospital plumbers. When we asked what it was, he said that he was making a game for us. He called it a "jungle-gym" and told us that we could climb on it any time we liked. None of us was really sure what to do and finally Dr Fry picked up Sunil and put him halfway up. He climbed slowly onto the top and then all of us had a try. At first we didn't think it was a very good game but afterwards we used it as a fort, or made believe that it was a truck or a tank. We used to make a lot of noise and the cook would tell us to keep quite, though Dr Fry didn't seem to mind. The next year, he made a swing for us from one of the branches of the gul mohur tree, with a rope tied to one of the old tyres from the ambulance, which was ripped on one side.

When I was very young, I remember there were other missionaries at the compound, the Barkers who lived in the bungalow which Mr Ezekiel now has, and Thurber sahib who always slept until noon and never seemed to do very much. He left the same year as the Barkers and after that it was only Miss Reynolds and Dr Fry. We knew all about the missionaries from their servants, how Thurber sahib used to drink in secret, from a bottle hidden amongst his shoes, and that Miss Reynolds ate nothing but porridge for dinner and Dr Fry slept without pyjamas. They lived amongst us on the compound, worshipped in the same church, greeted us each day and yet they were different, sahibs and miss-sahibs, aloof and separate. Mother says that some day they will all go back to America and we will have the compound to ourselves. But I am never sure of how she means these things, whether she actually wants them to leave or not.

We have always lived in Pipra. I was born at the hospital and grew up within the walls of the church compound, amongst my own people. The farthest I had ever been was the brick kiln to the south and never east of the town. To the north there lay the railway tracks which was our boundary and to the west of the compound was the canal. We never went beyond.

The canal was one of my favourite places. We would go fishing in the sluggish water, the tresses of weeds swirling in the current. Egrets and storks picked their way through the marsh grass, which grew along the edge. Fish turned in silver arcs upon the sandy bottom. We liked collecting the clams with their glossy mother-ofpearl casings, reflecting the sunlight as an oil stain, in rainbow colours. We played only on the near bank of the canal, swam only halfway across, as though on the other side there lay a crocodile, ready to snap us up. The near side was familiar, we knew every tree, as though they were our guardians. We climbed into their branches and squatted there like paddy-birds. We watched the ducks come floating down the canal and fired at them with our catapults.

Beyond the canal and southward lay the ravines, the tawny soil eroding into rivulets which grew wider and deeper until they gouged out twisting channels in the ground. The ravines were overgrown with thorns. Jackals skulked in front of their dens. We were told that anyone who wandered into the ravines would never come out again, for they were like a maze of passages which took you deeper and deeper inside. There was no escape from the ravines.

Following the canal bank, we would come back to the railway tracks. The trains crossed over a bridge of steel girders and carried on towards Gwalior and Delhi. We would walk along the diminishing perspective of the rails, stepping from sleeper to sleeper. We never tried to explore the empty fields which lay on the other side of the tracks. Something held us back, a kind of fear. From the high embankment, we could look across to the hospital, the compound, and the outskirts of Pipra. We could see the police lines and the firing range, tattered palms and half-constructed houses, the cold-storage plant and the jail. The landscape looked war-torn, though it has never seen a war in anyone's recollection, battle-scarred, though the last armies paraded here almost two hundred years ago.

There is nothing exotic about Pipra. There is nothing to stop and see, no forts with a lingering sense of power and magnificence, no natural splendour, no history. Pipra begins to appear on the milestones five miles out of town to the west and three miles out of town to the east. On the kilometre markers it is seven kilometres to the west and four to the east. Up until then Madinpur and Indore are the only distances given. Beyond these limits, Pipra doesn't exist.

The motor road divides the church compound from the hospital, a straight line of tar-coal bisecting our narrow world. There are hedgerows and trees on the compound and almost everyone has a garden. All of the people who work in the hospital live here, as well

84

as other Christian families, maybe eighty people altogether. Some of the bungalows have been divided so that two or three families live under the same roof. The only new building is the nurses' hostel which was built two years after I was born. Otherwise the nurses and the quarters go back almost a hundred years. Because of the tube well there is plenty of water and most of the compound is lush and green, except for a few months during summer. But overall there is feeling of neglect and disrepair. Only the church is freshly painted. In some ways the compound has become like a village. People have their cows and goats and chicken coops in the back yards. The hospital sweepers have a sounder of pigs which are always rooting up the gardens and causing trouble. There used to be a wall encircling the compound but it has fallen down in places and the bricks have been used for different things. In the outer corners of the compound, a jungle has grown up, with thorns and high grass. These were our secret places, where the crow-pheasant nests in the bamboo thicket. We played our hiding games in the scraggly growth of besharam booti, a plant which even the goats refuse to eat; it has big, limp blossoms, neither pink nor purple, dejected leaves and milky stalk. The compound is like an island on the edge of Pipra, a secluded sanctuary, unaffected by the outside world.

In that way, the hospital is very different. There is always something happening and people come from all around, not only Christians. When we were children the nurses never let us into the hospital unless we had a reason, but in the yard outside we would sit and listen to the men who brought their families in from the villages for treatment. Usually they talked of things which wouldn't interest us, land prices and water, the cost of cattle and seed, but now and again they would tell their hunting stories about leopards and bears and porcupines. We would sit close and listen as they told about the wounded bear that mauled a woodcutter who was brought to the hospital and how the doctors had sewed his face together again so that he had a different face and his wife wouldn't believe it was him.

Sometimes there would be an accident on the road and the ambulance would bring the injured to the hospital, bleeding and unable to walk. We would watch to see which ones survived and which of them died. There was a kind of excitement at the hospital which the compound never had, even though we hated it when our

85

mothers took us there for bandages or the time my knee swelled up with pus and Dr Fry had to drain it with a syringe. As a boy, I never stayed in the hospital, except when I was born, and afterwards I seldom went into the wards – once when my father had his appendix burst and the time Jojeph's cousin got so sick they thought he was going to die. Inside it was always dark and there was the pungent, sour smell of medicines, the whisper of voices and the sound of nurse's shoes on the cement floor.

It was much more interesting under the neem trees, listening to the stories. Some of the patients came outside to smoke. If Miss Reynolds caught them with a cigarette or bidi inside the hospital she would throw them out, even if they were halfway dead. They would come out in their pyjamas and squat down with the others and describe their pains and symptoms for anyone who asked. We would listen and wonder whether such things would ever happen to us.

Sometimes we sneaked around the back of the hospital to the garbage dump and the incinerator where the sweepers burnt all of the old bandages and the paper and threw out the broken instruments and glass. The sweepers would let us hunt for the rubber tubes which we used to make our catapults and the old syringes which we took and made into squirt pistols. Once we found a set of old X-rays which showed skulls and bones. There was one in which you could see exactly where the person's arm had been broken, just below the elbow. For a while we used to scavenge the dump every day for surgical gloves and laboratory slides, until Miss Reynolds finally caught us.

She was coming out of OPD with a large pair of forceps in her hand. When she saw what we were doing, she started to scream at us in her own particular Miss-sahib Hindi, telling us that we should get out of there "jhut put" and we were all "budmash" and "shaitani" and if she ever caught us there again, she'd "danda le kar marega", and we must "chaley jao ek dum". Miss Reynolds came after us, waving the forceps over her head, but by then we were away and running. Later, from the cover of the lantana bushes behind the hospital, we could hear her giving it to the sweepers for letting us go near the garbage dump. After that we only went back one at a time, when we knew she wasn't there and all we really wanted were the rubber tubes for our catapults.

FOUR

I HAD GONE to the canal for fishing. It was the monsoon season but there had hardly been any rain. Getting up at dawn, I dug worms from the rosebeds near the church. Kapil had said that he would come with me but I knew that he would never wake up. The sky was overcast, though the clouds were far above the earth and it did not look as though it would rain, except in the hills. The water in the canal was a chalky brown, with flecks of mica which glistened when the current swirled up in eddies near the pillars of the bridge. I knew there were several large fish there. One of them had broken my line the day before. Even though it was still half-dark when I arrived at the bridge, the air was hot and moist. There was a putrid smell, the stench of something dead.

I settled myself at the best place, just where the steps came down from the canal bridge and there was a platform for bathing. The water was deepest there. I had made a float from the quill of a peacock feather and baiting my hook, I tossed it out gently and let the current draw the line through my fingers. I squatted there like this for almost an hour and when the light grew brighter I saw a dead cat floating in the shallow water near the far bank, its fur matted and its belly swollen up. That was where the smell had been coming from. The sun was just breaking through the clouds, dusting the acacia trees with light. A flock of egrets flew overhead, their white wings pumping the air. It was getting hotter and I had given up hope of catching any fish.

Just then, I looked upstream and saw a woman walking towards me along the bank of the canal. She was far away, but I could tell that she was in some kind of trouble. There was nobody with her and she was carrying a bundle in her arms. The way she walked, I knew that she had come a long distance on foot and she was tired. But there was a determined, almost trance-like rhythm to her steps, as though she was mad or sick. Something about her made me feel afraid. I could see by her clothes that she was a tribal woman, a girl really, only a few years older than myself. Her hair was braided loosely at the back but it had come undone and there were strands falling across her face. She was crying.

Reeling in my line, I wrapped it around the wooden spindle which I used for fishing. The float danced over the water as I pulled it in. By now, I could see that the woman was carrying a child in her arms. The baby was very still and I thought it might be dead. I crouched there by the water, watching as she went past. The woman stared straight ahead of her and didn't look at me. Her eyes were glazed with tears and the headscarf which all tribal women wear was dragging on the ground. I could tell that something terrible had happened. Her face was streaked with tears but it was not twisted and ugly, the way some people get when they cry. Instead there was a blank expression on the woman's face which seemed much worse. I could remember when old Mr Samuel died, how the compound women gathered in his courtyard and howled all night. I didn't think it sounded as though they were really sad. This woman went past me silently and when she came to the bridge, turned left towards the hospital.

Something about the woman made me follow her. I did not go too close but stayed about a hundred yards behind, watching as she walked straight on, keeping to the unpaved side of the road. She had no shoes and from behind I could see that she was limping slightly. As soon as she reached the hospital, the woman turned at the gate and went inside.

It was still quite early in the morning and the night nurses were just coming off duty. The chowkidar tried to stop the woman at the entrance but she walked past him and seeing the child, he let her through.

For me, she was like a figure out of a terrible dream, a sad and mournful woman, her clothes in tatters. I was not sure whether the child was alive or dead but there was an overwhelming sense of tragedy about the woman. I had carried the worms with me, wrapped up in an old scrap of newspaper and I could feel them crawling out between my fingers. Flinging them into the ditch near the hospital gate, I hurried home.

Villagers came to the hospital from all around, mostly tribals. They often arrived at night, walking, or sometimes in a cart. Along the road outside the gate of the hospital they would set up camp, and in the morning when we went to school we would see them sitting in groups around a fire or gathering dry sticks from the bushes at the edge of the compound. They were different from us and spoke

88

another dialect so that I could only catch a word or two of what they said. To me there was always something disturbing about their faces, their eyes, the way they watched us walking off to school, our bookbags slung across our shoulders. I knew that they came from the forests beyond the mountains, a place where I had never been. They were hunters mostly, and many of them had their spears and dogs. I used to imagine myself going out with them into the forest and stalking deer and peacocks, tracking wild boar through the high grass.

For the tribals our hospital was something strange and mysterious, just as their forests and mountains were to us. They would sit patiently outside the gate, afraid to go inside until one of the chowkidars called to them. Whenever the nurses and doctors walked across from the church compound, they would stand up and fold their hands respectfully, as if just by seeing the doctors in their white coats and the nurses in their starched uniforms, they might be cured.

Once, Kapil and I watched a group of tribals catching pigeons in a well. It was amazing how simple they made it seem. Nearby the hospital there were a number of abandoned wells which had gone dry and filled with mud. The brick sides had fallen down and they were overgrown with thorns. Pigeons and swallows nested in the wells and I had often seen them flying out and back in the evenings. One day Kapil and I had gone out to the maidan beyond the hospital to see if there were any rabbits about. At a distance, I noticed three men standing by a well and going closer, we could see that they had covered the mouth of the well with a blanket. As I watched, one of the two younger men climbed inside. The others waited above, smoking patiently and holding down the edges of the blanket. After a while, the man came out of the well. In one hand, he had four pigeons. They were still alive and he was holding them by the wings so that they fluttered awkwardly. The other two men lifted the blanket off the well and folded it. Two more pigeons flew out and away into the sky. The three men built a fire near the well and roasted the pigeons right there. I don't think they had eaten for several days.

The men had brought an old woman to the hospital that morning. She was very sick and the day before I had seen them carrying her on a litter made of bamboo poles. She was lying still as a corpse, wrapped in the same blanket which they had used to trap

89

the pigeons. After she had been admitted to the hospital, the men had made a temporary shelter for themselves at one edge of the compound, using an old piece of tarpaulin they had been given by Dr Fry. As usual we had kept our distance. My mother and the other ladies of the compound always warned us about the tribals, telling us of all the terrible things they did, sacrificing children to the goddess and burning themselves with fiery brands. We had been strictly told never to speak with them, for they were dangerous and unpredictable. They were wild people of the forest and came from beyond the limits of our world, from beyond the railway tracks and the canal, out of the shadows of the mountains.

By the afternoon everyone on the compound had heard about the woman I had seen. When we asked the nurses, they said that the baby was a girl; she was very weak and sick with an infection. They were sure that she was going to die. One of the nurses had to sit beside the crib all day and through the night. The mother could not feed her and the girl was too weak to drink from a bottle, so they had to use a medicine dropper. For two days everyone kept talking about the baby and since the next day was Sunday, my father prayed for her life in church, asking that she should be spared. By Monday night, she was better and the fever had come down. Miss Reynolds said it was a miracle that the baby had lived. Dr Fry had made a special formula with condensed milk and water which the girl had finally sucked from a bottle and very soon the nurses said that she was out of danger.

The mother stayed in the hall outside the nursery. The nurses tried to give her a place to sleep in one of the wards but she refused to leave the doorway. It was only when the baby started getting better that she told her story and we learned something about her past. Her name was Mamta and she came from a village to the east. She was a widow, even though she was just a girl. Mamta didn't know her own age exactly and she said that her husband had died a few months after her marriage. She had gone back to live with her own family but they did not want her because of the baby which she was going to have. All of this, she told to the duty nurses when they asked her and we heard the story from them.

After the first day, when I saw her walking along the canal road, I didn't see Mamta again for more than a week. Nobody was quite sure what would happen to her once the baby was well again. She didn't have anywhere to go and when the nurses asked her if she wanted to return to her village, she was very determined not to go back. In the end, Mrs Abraham Lal offered to keep her as a servant and let her stay in the little store room at the back of her house. The baby was better now and Miss Reynolds gave her tinned milk with which to feed the child, and bottles too. Mamta seemed quite happy working for Mrs Abraham Lal and we would see her sweeping out the angan and washing the pots and pans at the tap, scrubbing them with ash until they gleamed. She was happy now and we made friends with her quite easily. The baby grew stronger with the milk and Mamta would make a hammock for her out of a shawl and tie it under the gul mohur tree and rock the baby to sleep. She would come outdoors to shell peas or pick clean the rice. She learned our names and asked us what we studied at school. Mamta wanted us to teach her how to write and we would scratch the alphabet in the dust for her to copy. Mrs Abraham Lal said that she worked hard and she was clean and even though she did not pay her but only gave her meals and the room, Mamta was quite happy.

One of the nurses gave her a new sari and others gave Mamta clothes for herself and the baby. They felt sorry for her and she accepted what they gave her with a look of surprise as though she had never expected so much kindness. Mamta was always bathed and clean, not at all like the first time I saw her walking along the canal bank, with her hair in tangles and her face smudged with tears. Though she was dark skinned, there was something very beautiful about Mamta, the way her eyes and teeth shone. She would climb into the neem tree next to our house each morning and break a twig with which she scrubbed her teeth, chewing one end into a brush and spitting out the bits of bark.

Though we had seen many tribals at the hospital and in the town, Mamta was the first to live amongst us. We were curious and asked her many questions about her village and the forests where she had grown up. She would tell us about her grandfather, who was a great hunter and once killed a leopard with an axe. Mamta taught us how to make snares to catch rabbits, though we never succeeded. She said that we didn't have the patience to be real hunters. She knew all about different plants, which ones to use if we had cut ourselves, to stop the bleeding, and which leaves to rub on our skin if we had itching and how to make a special brew of bark and berries to cure a stomach ache. We played all kinds of games around the compound, in the overgrown areas near the wall of the graveyard. If she finished her work, sometimes Mamta would come with us to the bamboo thicket and pretend that we were living in the jungle. She knew how to light a fire so easily, just a whisp of grass and a few dry twigs. Sitting there in our secret hideaway, Mamta would tell us stories which she had heard from childhood, about ghosts and animals. She took her little girl with her wherever she went, never letting the child out of her sight.

We would play with Mamta's daughter and let her clutch our fingers, hold her high above our heads, so that she laughed and laughed. We asked Mamta what her name would be, but she said that she had not yet thought of one. She called her nonsense names, softly whispering in the baby's ear. I never heard the girl crying, only whimper to go back to her mother when we had held her for too long. Mamta was not more than a year older than Binu, maybe sixteen or seventeen, and it was as though she were one of us, not a grown-up woman like our mothers but a girl with whom we played. The only difference was that her doll was real, unlike the cotton and plastic babies which the other girls would carry about, knitting tiny sweaters for them and frocks made out of handkerchiefs. Mamta's doll was alive and I remember the time that Jojeph was holding her and she peed all over him. We laughed so hard, I had tears in my eyes.

FIVE

IT WAS SEVERAL months after she arrived in Pipra that Mamta took
me to the fair. Though she usually carried her daughter with her
wherever she went, this time Mamta left the girl asleep at home.
One of the nurses had offered to look after her for an hour or two.
Mamta had asked some of the other children to come with us, Binu,
Kapil and Sunil, but their parents had not allowed them and I felt
fortunate to be going alone with Mamta, just the two of us. There
was something very exciting about the fair, a sort of forbidden,
anxious feeling. It lay outside the boundaries of our compound,
beyond the railway tracks and the canal. It was something from
another world and I'm sure that if my parents had known that the
other children were not going they would never have given me
permission. To them the fair was something crude and un-
Christian. It was like the cinema halls. Bad sorts of people went to
fairs.

As we set out, Mamta and I walked hurriedly, an eagerness to our
steps. Without her child, Mamta seemed much closer to my age,
more carefree and lighthearted. In the darkness, I felt so close to
her. I wanted to keep on walking with Mamta, further and further
away from home, escaping together, further than anywhere I had
ever gone before, up into the shadow of the mountains. I wanted to
run away with Mamta and never come back.

As we came to the gate of the fairground I began to feel afraid. It
was so strange and different. I felt as though it was not Pipra but
another town, the harshness of the music, the crowds of people
pushing their way amongst the stalls, the jugglers and acrobats, the
garish tents and brilliant lights, a fierce whirl of faces, arms and
hands.

When I saw the circus with its large sign, advertising the beast, I
did not want to go inside, but at the same time I did not want
Mamta to know that I was frightened. She paid for us and I
followed her into the tent, feeling as though there was something
holding me back, tugging at the collar of my shirt, a hollow, uneasy
feeling.

93

And what we discovered inside was unlike anything that I'd expected – siamese twins in a bottle. At first it seemed to me like something sinful and obscene. But then I saw Mamta bowing down in front of it and I realized that she had kept a part of herself hidden from the others, a side to her which they would never accept. The beast no longer seemed so hideous and deformed, but something very real and even beautiful, the most perfect creature in the world.

Mamta was supposed to be very good at giving massage and my mother called her in to rub her knees, which were always paining her. Mamta would squat down on the ground and dip her hands in oil and press my mother's legs for half an hour each day. Whenever she came to our house, Mamta would bring the girl and let me play with her. The girl could hardly crawl and I would carry her around the angan, pointing to different things and telling her the names.

My mother and Mamta would talk together and mother would tell her about the hospital and the compound. She would also ask Mamta about Mrs Abraham Lal and how much she spent on food each week and whether her son smoked at home, questions which made Mamta laugh. Mrs Abraham Lal's son was the X-ray technician at the hospital, an arrogant, unpleasant man. Last year, one of the nurses had to leave because of him. Mamta would tell us how terrible he was and how he drank too much. She said he sometimes even beat his mother. Mamta's hands were strong and agile, moving over my mother's legs with a smooth and graceful rhythm, like a potter moulding clay. Sometimes my mother would make a sound, if she pressed too hard. She said that after Mamta had massaged her knees, they were always better for an hour or two.

There was talk that Mamta might become a Christian. Mrs Abraham Lal began to teach her from the Bible and Mamta used to ask us questions about Jesus and Mary. Once she asked why Jesus made people drink his blood and we all laughed and said it wasn't real blood, only grape juice, and then she was puzzled. We told her the stories which we knew from the Bible – David and the giant, the flood and about Samson who never cut his hair. In return, Mamta would tell us stories about her village in the forest and the goddess who was born from a knot in a tree. She told us about children who were lost in the forest and adopted by wolves. She told us about the white cobra that lived in a ruined temple and how the villagers left bowls of milk for it to drink, and the time her grandfather shot a wild bear and when he finished skinning it, the animal got to its feet and ran away, just like a man. She told us about the cocoons she gathered in the trees and the moths with eyes on their wings that flew away to the moon and the spiders' webs across the paths in the forest. Whoever broke the webs was cursed forever. At night the spiders would search them out and smother them to death.

Each Sunday Mamta would come to church and sit at the back and listen to the hymns and prayers. The baby would lie quietly asleep in her lap. Mrs Abraham Lal gave her some coloured pictures from the Bible which she would show us and ask for explanations.

Mamta also went to several prayer meetings as well but we were not allowed at these. The adults would go to Miss Reynolds's bungalow and kneel down in a circle and pray. There was one of the nurses who had come from Jabalpur, Sister Miriam, who was able to speak in tongues. My father disapproved of her but he was obliged to go to the prayer meetings and mother and he would leave the house dressed in their Sunday clothes, though father never wore his cassock to the prayer meetings.

Mamta would tell us about it afterwards and I was never sure whether she found it funny or took it seriously because sometimes she laughed, when she told us how Miriam started throwing herself around and about the way they laid their hands on her head and prayed to God, or the time Mrs Abraham Lal started to cry out loud and asked God for a new X-ray machine for the hospital. Her son was always complaining that the machine was no good.

I don't remember anyone else being converted and we were eager to see my father baptize Mamta and her daughter. We wondered whether she would change her name. I wondered if Mamta would become like the other compound ladies. In some ways I didn't want her to become like us. I wanted her to remain a tribal girl, with her own beliefs and stories. I wanted her to stay that way. I was afraid that once Mamta became a Christian she would no longer play with us or tell us stories about the goddess and the snake. I wondered if she would remove the amulet from around her neck and the nose ring too. There was surely no way that she could get rid of the tattoos from her hands and arms. They were like ink stains on her dark skin, like the pattern of needle marks which old Mr. Samuel used to have on his arm because he was a diabetic and had to take injections every day.

Mamta came to see my father and Mrs Abraham Lal came with her. They sat in the angan and talked about the Bible while the baby sat with me in my room. She was crawling now and used to drag herself along the ground, making strange burbling noises. I tried to think of a good Christian name for her like Mary or Amanda, those were the names of the Barker's daughters and I thought how nice they sounded. My mother made tea for Mamta, treating her differently now that she was going to become a Christian. I wondered if mother would still have Mamta press her legs, after she'd converted.

My mother gave Mamta one of her saris to wear for the baptism. It was a pale cream silk with red flowers on the border. She took it out of an old trunk under her bed and told Mamta to iron it carefully. There was a tear in one corner and Mamta darned it up so that it hardly showed. Everyone was excited about the baptism. I remember that my father said something about Mamta being, "a bride of Christ," and I imagined her wearing mother's sari and walking down the aisle of the church like a real bride at a wedding and my father standing at the altar with his hands raised and everyone singing hymns of joy.

It was the end of winter, and two days before Mamta was going to be baptized there was a terrible andhi, a dust storm. I stood on top of our roof and watched it coming. At first there was nothing but a yellow smear across the sky. There was an iridescent quality about it, not quite like a sunset, which has a sudden brilliance, gradually fading into grey. The andhi instead had a ·glimmering light as though all of the particles in the air had come to life. Soon, the whole sky was yellow, a mustard colour. In the distance there was a howl. My father had gone into town and only my mother and I were in the house.

I stood on the roof for a long time and watched as the palm trees far away and south of the town were suddenly batted about by the wind. One minute they were straight and still and then in an instant they were bent double. The fury of the andhi was not so frightening as the feeling of gathering violence, the jaundiced light of the sky and the shadowy expanse of blowing sand which followed the

96

wind. I could see the smoke-stacks at the brick kiln standing out stark and menacing in the eerie light. The brick kiln had not been used for several years, not since Mr Samson had been caught. As the wind reached the kiln, I saw the smoke-stacks shudder and then suddenly one of them rose up out of the ground and toppled over. The sound of the wind was too loud to hear the crash and it almost seemed to happen in silence, the other smoke-stack bending under the force of the wind and also crashing down. Now I could see a wave of sand, billowing across the jheel. The electric wires, a quarter mile away, suddenly arched against their poles. There was a white flash of light, a crackling of electricity, as one of the wires snapped and shorted against the rest. The lights in our house went off. I heard my mother calling and ran down stairs.

"Gideon," she shouted. "Bolt the windows."

The moaning of the storm was deep and resonant. I heard my mother banging shut the windows in the kitchen. The wind hit us and the walls shuddered. I struggled with the angan door and finally got it closed. For a moment there was just the wind, like heavy breathing outside.

Then the sand and grit lashed against the house. It sounded like rain or hail and came in sheets. I heard a cry from inside and rushed to see what had happened. The angan was a whirlpool of sand, sucking against the windows. A brass water vessel had been knocked over and was rolling about on the floor, making a hollow, ringing noise. My mother cried again. She was inside the kitchen. A step ladder had fallen down and wedged itself into the door frame. That and the force of the wind, trapped her inside. I made my way along the wall, my eyes winced shut against the dust and sand which stung my face like a swarm of insects.

I struggled with the ladder and finally pulled it loose. From inside, my mother pushed the door open. The blast of the storm almost threw her back into the kitchen. Shielding my eyes, I grabbed her hand and dragged her across the angan to the drawing-room. She sat down on the sofa and covered her face with her hands while I bolted the door.

Inside the room there was an oppressive feeling. I could feel the sand on my lips and teeth. The lights were off and with the windows shut it was quite dark. The wind seeped into the room through the cracks and there were little drifts of sand forming next to the window sills. Somewhere in the house one of the screens had come loose and was clapping open and shut. The drawing-room seemed to be at the eye of the storm and despite the constant howling outside the walls, there was a silence within.

The storm went on for almost an hour and at the end it began to rain. The sound changed from the grating of the sand against the windows to the soft splatter of raindrops and immediately the rasping dryness of the storm was replaced by the sweet odour of wet earth. The air changed and the threatening atmosphere was gone. The wind too died away and the clouds looked bruised and swollen when I opened the door and looked out. In the distance, I could hear thunder but the storm had passed beyond us now and there was a peaceful calm.

Our angan was littered with leaves and broken sticks from the neem trees. One of the earthen pots which my mother used for storing water had shattered and I could see that the clothes lines which we had strung on the roof had blown down along with their bamboo supports. Even though it was still raining lightly, I went outside to look at everything which had been destroyed. The chimneys at the brick kiln were bent and crumpled. There was an unreal feeling after the storm, a contrast between such sudden violence and now the stillness and the fresh perfume of the rain. I could see that one of the large eucalyptus trees at the far end of the compound had been uprooted. There was damage everywhere. Mrs Soloman's chicken coop had been torn apart, bits and pieces strewn about the yard. The hens were huddled under a bush. Going round the compound, I saw that several mulberry trees had fallen down and one of the electric poles near Miss Reynolds's bungalow. There were wires lying all about. I found a dead myna lying near the tube well, its wings open, as if it had died in mid-flight, battling against the wind. Part of the church roof had come off, the corrugated tin sheets which covered the front half of the building. Everybody had come outdoors to see the damage. The bougainvilleas had been in bloom and now the petals were strewn everywhere like drops of blood. I didn't go across to the hospital but I heard that the water heating system which Dr Fry had built on the roof had blown away completely and one of the pieces had landed in the wheat fields, a hundred yards away.

In the middle of all this confusion, I heard somebody say that

Mamta had been hurt. I ran across to Mrs Abraham Lal's house and saw that there was a crowd at the doorway. Two of the nurses had been called and I could hear the baby crying. When I tried to push my way inside, somebody held me back and told me to go away. Binu was there and she said that Mrs Abraham Lal had been over at the hospital visiting one of the patients and when she came back after the storm, she found Mamta in her room, lying in the corner, unconscious. The baby was sitting on the bed and crying. Mamta had cut her forehead and there was blood all over her clothes. Nobody knew what could have happened since she was indoors and everything was closed up tightly.

We stood outside the door, wondering what was happening when after a while two men came running with a stretcher from the hospital and they went inside. Everyone seemed anxious and afraid. The storm had been forgotten and people were trying to find out what had happened. One person said it might have been lightning or maybe she had been outside and got hit by one of the falling trees. Mamta could have crawled into the house and then collapsed.

The men carried her out on the stretcher and I could tell that she was awake, though her head was turned away from me. One of the nurses was holding her hand and they had wrapped Mamta in a blanket. The other nurse was holding the baby. Mrs Abraham Lal was crying. Nobody seemed to know what was wrong and we all followed the stretcher as they carried Mamta to the hospital where Dr Fry was waiting at the entrance. One of the chowkidars was holding a lantern because the lights were off. Just as they took her inside, it began to rain more heavily and we had to run back to our houses.

In the evening when I asked my mother about Mamta, she got very angry. She told me that I was always too curious and there was nothing I needed to know. Mother seemed very upset and when I went to bed, I could hear her telling my father what had happened. Her voice was low and I couldn't get the words, but from her tone I knew that something terrible had been done to Mamta. I was confused and didn't understand why she would be so secretive. I couldn't see the reason for her to get angry with my questions. The way she talked with father frightened me and I could not sleep that night, imagining Mamta in the storm, the dust blowing about her and the trees crashing down on all sides as she ran from one end of the compound to the other, trying to find a place to hide. The next morning I got up and went outside without even washing my face, before my mother could stop me. I wanted to see Mamta and learn the truth of what had happened. It was early and there was nobody about. The storm had passed completely and there were only the fallen trees to remind me of the wind and sand. I ran as fast as I could to the hospital. Sister Tara was standing outside. She was one of the nicer nurses and I knew she was a friend of Mamta's.

"How is she?" I said. "Is she all right?"

Sister Tara looked at me with a sad expression.

"Was she hurt too badly?" I said.

"Mamta's gone," said Sister Tara.

At first I thought she meant that she was dead.

"Gideon, go home. She's gone."

"Gone where?" I said.

Sister Tara shook her head.

"She went away. Maybe she's gone back to her village. I don't know."

"But why?" I said. "Wasn't she hurt?"

"Don't ask me silly questions, Gideon," she said. "Go home. It doesn't matter now."

She turned quickly to go inside.

"Did she take her daughter?" I said.

Sister Tara looked back at me and shook her head. I could see that she was crying now, the tears running down her face.

People didn't talk about it afterwards the way they did with Mr Samson and Ruth or the other things that happened on the compound. It was as though everyone was afraid to mention Mamta after she had left. I knew that Mrs Abraham Lal's son had something to do with it. Binu had seen him running into the house just before the storm. A few weeks afterwards he went away from Pipra. Everyone was glad that he had gone. Nobody said it, but I knew that he had done something to Mamta and it wasn't the storm at all that hurt her. It was him. Binu seemed to know the most and she told me how he'd hit her with a spade and cut her head, besides the other things he'd done. I could imagine her in the room. Nobody could hear her cries as he attacked her, knocking her to the ground and lying over her in a way that I could only imagine as a picture I had seen once in a magazine which Kapil showed me, two bodies locked together like the child in the bottle, struggling, a beast, a monster and Mamta prostrate on the ground, the ugliness of it all and the violence of the storm.

Mamta left our lives as abruptly as she arrived and with that same sense of tragedy and betrayal, so terrible I wanted to go and fling myself into the canal and drown. It was as if I had no reason to live any more. She abandoned me in the same way she abandoned her daughter. I could not get away from the memory of the first time I saw Mamta walking along the canal bank, carrying the baby in her arms, that inescapable feeling of despair. I couldn't forget the emptiness of her eyes, the way she walked past me and the stench of the dead cat, the oppressive heat that morning as I followed her and the worms oozing through my fingers.

Nobody heard of Mamta after she left the compound, but there was a feeling which I used to get once in a while when I was walking along the canal bank or when I heard bicycles going by in the dark or the call of the crow pheasant; I used to imagine that Mamta was close at hand watching us from the cover of some bush. She had never actually left us but was only hiding somewhere in the shadows of the compound wall or just beyond the limits of the railway tracks and the canal. She was waiting for me to find her as if it were some kind of hiding game.

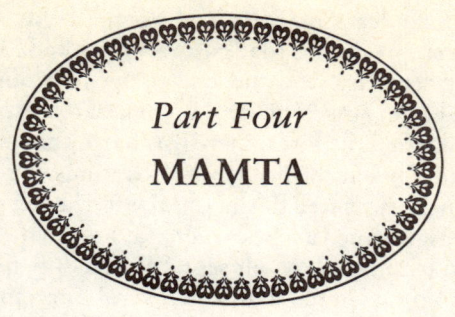

Part Four
MAMTA

ONE

THEY HAD to push the Studebaker to get it started. Dr Fry sat
behind the wheel pumping the accelerator and tugging at the choke.
Finally, the fourth time they pushed it down the length of the
driveway, the engine caught with a hoarse gurgle and started up. A
blue cloud of smoke billowed out of the exhaust pipe. Tricia stood
sweating and coughing, while Fry revved the engine and got the
Studebaker turned around. There were seven of them altogether, as
well as the boxes of medicine and equipment which were loaded in
the trunk and on the roof. Tricia got into the front seat with one of
the nurses. She had to straddle a wicker basket which contained
their picnic lunch and several thermos flasks of tea and coffee. Fry
grinned at her as she squeezed into the seat beside him.

He was wearing a baseball hat which gave him a jaunty, youthful
air. Fry jammed the gear shift into first. They started off with a lot
of vibration as if the car was going to explode. Tricia held her
breath. The nurse sat scrubbed and starched beside her, hands
folded on her knees. Tricia tried to think of something to say and
then gave up the thought of conversation. She had brought her
camera to take pictures of the village. They drove along the motor
road for some distance, through scattered farmland and open
jungle.

"You see that line of hills over there," said Fry. "That's where
we're headed."

"How long will it take?" asked Tricia.

"Another half an hour," said Fry, swinging the car off the paved road onto a dusty track which cut across the fields. "Fortunately the rains have stopped. This road can get pretty bad sometimes. We got stuck out here last year and had to spend the night under a mango tree. The next morning it took a pair of oxen to pull us out."

Once they entered the forest there was hardly any road at all. Dr Fry drove carefully but the Studebaker's springs were not the best and by the time they neared the mountains Tricia felt as though she was rattling just as much as the car. Fry sat hunched over the wheel and she could tell that every jolt sent a spasm of pain up his back. There were deep ruts in the road and several times the car scraped bottom. Dust seeped in through the holes in the floor and cracks in the windows. Trying to keep from being thrown about, Tricia braced her hand on the top of the dashboard.

Kaproli was a small village of fifteen or twenty huts bunched together on a barren hill, surrounded by jungle. There was a small stream running past, bordered on either side by a margin of round white rocks. Dr Fry veered off the track about two hundred yards before the village and parked the car under a clump of trees which grew beside the stream. Before he'd even switched the engine off, a swarm of tiny figures came racing down the hill towards them. For a moment Tricia was startled, thinking that they were pygmies, until she noticed one or two adults appear at the edge of the village. The children were mostly naked and they were carrying sticks or bows and arrows. From a distance they could have been mistaken for a tribe of miniature people, racing down to defend their village. Along with them were several barking dogs.

Fry got out and stretched his back. Tricia dusted off her clothes. Even the nurse in her spotless uniform looked dishevelled from the drive. The men began unloading the car and within a few minutes the Studebaker was transformed into a make-shift dispensary. The front seat was taken out, wiped and dusted, and a clean sheet spread over the torn upholstery to create an examining couch. The flat hood of the car was also draped with a sheet and became a table on which they arranged different bottles of medicine, instruments and bandages. The trunk was opened and more boxes were brought out along with a couple of folding chairs. The back of the car was turned into a washing area with two jerrycans of water, an enamel basin, mugs, soap and disinfectant.

There were only forty inhabitants in Kaproli, but people came to the clinic from all around. Some patients would walk eight or ten miles for treatment and there were times when so many came that they were forced to work late into the night, using hurricane lanterns. Fry had once removed a tumour from a woman's abdomen, operating by the headlights of the Studebaker. He had spent so many years working under these conditions that nothing seemed unusual and the impossible became routine. He was proud of his skill and ability to make do with the simplest instruments. He knew there was no gadgetry which could match his own two hands.

By now the children had gathered around in a circle, brandishing their weapons with curiosity.

"How often do you come out here?" asked Tricia, as Fry was washing up.

"Once a month or so," said Fry. "We've got several other places where we hold our clinics and we try to visit one village each week."

"You must have been coming here for a long time," she said.

"Almost ten years. Before that, we used to make longer trips for several days at a time, but after awhile, with a shortage of staff at the hospital, we had to give it up."

"Can't these people come to the hospital?" asked Tricia.

"They do, some of them, but it's still a distance and if it's something minor, they'll wait until it's really serious, infected, fatal sometimes. This way we can catch the little things before they get out of hand. Also, people are sometimes scared of a hospital for a lot of reasons. That's why we always hold our clinics in the open so that everybody can see what's happening. There's nothing to hide."

An old man with a white moustache, yellowed by tobacco stains, came around the back of the car and greeted Fry with folded hands. He was frail and obsequious but Fry welcomed him with a respectful salute. Tricia listened as they spoke in Hindustani. He was the head man of Kaproli.

". . . and the biggest hypochondriac you've ever known," said Fry, after he had introduced Tricia to the old man. "He's probably healthier than half the village put together but he's been insisting that he's about to die for as long as I can remember."

The dogs which had been barking when they first arrived were now circling the ambulance, sniffing at the tyres. They were pied and gaunt, with thin, narrow faces. Tricia knelt down and snapped her fingers at them. The dogs cringed and slowly came towards her. She couldn't help but feel pity for them, with their ribs showing and their hollow flanks. Tricia noticed that the headman of Kaproli was watching her with amusement as she scratched the dogs behind their ears and patted their heads. They responded with the dumb, unsuspecting love of animals. Tricia wished that she had something with which to feed them, a crust of bread or a cookie. Just then, the dogs spotted something at the edge of the forest and they set off barking frantically in that direction.

Having nothing to do, Tricia wandered down to the stream. She wished that she could help somehow, but Fry and the others had everything down to a routine and Tricia felt as though she would only be getting in the way. Besides, she wanted to be by herself. The stream was clear but the pools along the bank were covered with green scum and gave off a fœtid odour. The sky was overcast with ruffled banks of clouds and the air was heavy with moisture.

Tricia was disappointed by the village. She had hoped that they would be in the mountains but the shadowy ridges were still a distance off and the line of hills which Fry had pointed out was really nothing more than a rolling, uneven stretch of ground. The camera hung around her neck but Kaproli was hardly picturesque. It was squalid and unattractive. There was a heap of dung and twigs on one side. The huts were more like temporary shelters and several of them seemed ready to collapse. Next to the stream were a few dusty fields surrounded by a fence of dried branches and thorns.

It wasn't long before the children found her. Tricia was sitting on a large, white rock, tossing pebbles into the stream. They approached so silently that she didn't see them until they were only a few feet away. Again they startled her with their appearance. Most of them had long hair which was uncombed and matted, a rusty colour. Their faces were those of adults, with serious eyes and stern, unsmiling lips. All of the children were covered with dust and ash, especially on their legs and arms. Their stomachs were distended and their skin was a grey unhealthy colour.

Tricia remembered a poster from Sunday School, which hung on the wall in the basement of their church. It was a seductive picture of a city park, a squirrel in a maple tree, a fresh green lawn with dandelions. Christ was seated on a bench, surrounded by children. He seemed to glow with health and righteousness, a young man with blonde hair and beard, looking something like a well-groomed hippie in a shapeless robe, with sandals on his feet. The children were running up to him, their gleaming faces full of smiles. They were all so wholesome and well behaved, a Sunday School class from somewhere in the indeterminate American past. She had never seen such children, so clean, so happy to see their Saviour. The garden itself was almost surreal, some artist's conception of a suburban Gethsemani, the care with which each dandelion had been drawn, the wrought iron bench, the maples and conifers. There was something perverse about the picture, as if the colours were too real, the images too finely drawn. Underneath there was the scripture verse, the only words from the Bible that Tricia could remember, "Suffer the little children to come unto me . . ."

Tricia stared back at the semi-circle of tiny figures who surrounded her and wondered to herself what games they played. She thought of her own childhood and then tried to imagine herself as one of them.

She remembered when she was eight or ten, playing in the snow with Fritz. These children had never seen snow, she thought. Tricia loved the winter, sleds and snowmen, the ploughs coming past their house, the bleached white landscapes and blackened trees, snowballs with maple syrup which always made her teeth ache. It seemed like an impossible fantasy amidst the damp, warm air, the tropical forest, the thatch huts and naked children. Hartford was so far away – the snowflakes drifting down outside her window, the silence, stepping out into the yard, clean as a nuptial sheet, the first footprints circling out to the bird feeder and back. Tricia always felt happiest in winter. She and Fritz would make a snowman, rolling up great, huge balls of snow and smoothing them with their mittens. The snowman would stand in the yard like a sentry all winter long. They would put sticks for arms and a broom in his hand, a carrot for a nose (Fritz never had much imagination) and an old felt hat.

Tricia glanced around her at the pools of scummy water, the round white rocks and the idle stream. Getting up, she put her camera carefully on the ground and then caught sight of a stone which lay half-buried in the sand. Beckoning to the children, she began to dig around it with her hands.

"Come on, help me," she said, but all they did was stare.

Finally, Tricia freed the rock and with a lot of prying and pushing, she was able to roll it over. It was the perfect size. Eagerly, she gestured for the children to help her shift the stone to the rock where she'd been sitting. One or two of the older boys joined in and they were able to move it across. Lifting the stone was much more difficult, but by now all of the children were helping and they finally got it up on top of the larger rock. Tricia began to look around for a third. Going upstream with the children, she finally chose a smaller stone, about the size of a pumpkin. Two of the boys helped her lift it and accompanied by shouts and cries of encouragement, they were able to place it on top of the other two. All three stones were a greyish white.

By the time she'd finished, there was perspiration pouring down her face. Tricia felt pleased with what she'd made. The children were puzzled but they were smiling now and laughing. Tricia scooped up a handful of clay from the edge of the stream. It was a blackish colour. Very carefully she added the finishing touches, dabbing the stones with bits of mud. She searched around for a couple of forked sticks which she jammed between the upper and middle stones. By now the children had recognized that she was making the figure of a man and they were sitting round with gleeful expressions on their faces. Tricia retrieved her camera and took their picture, which delighted them even more.

Having heard the shouts and cries, Dr Fry came over to the edge of the stream-bed to see what was going on. She heard him laugh and for a moment the two of them just looked at each other. Fry took off his baseball hat and tossed it down to her.

"I never thought I'd see a snowman in Kaproli," he said, with a laugh.

Tricia put the hat on the snow man's head and smiled to herself.

The children tried to make another stone man on their own and she watched them struggle with the boulders, using their sticks as levers and splashing about in the shallow water. After awhile they lost interest and settled down beside her once again, as if waiting for her to think of another game.

"Will you take me up there?" said Tricia, pointing to the village. She was curious to see what the huts were like. At first the children did not understand what she was saying but after a little while they caught on and led her up the hill.

They climbed the dusty path which was pock-marked with the hoof prints of goats. Up close, Kaproli looked even less inviting. The huts seemed as though they had been put together overnight with thatch and twigs. There was an overwhelming stench of dung in the village. Most of the animals were out in the forest grazing, attended by the older children. Flies hovered over the filthy pools of water in the narrow spaces between the huts. The smoke, which drifted in feathery spirals from the thatch, had a sour, resinous smell. Each of the doorways was just large enough for the children and even Tricia would have had to stoop to enter. The huts seemed dark and airless inside. On one of the walls there were strange white markings, the smudged print of a hand, a crude drawing of the sun and other pictures which she couldn't recognize. On some of the thatch roofs there were squash and cucumber vines. A woman came out of one of the doorways, looked at Tricia for a moment and then ducked back into her hut without a word.

The children posed in front of an old, rusted hand-pump which lay against the wall of one of the houses. They insisted that Tricia take their picture, very proud of the pump even though it was useless. One of the boys worked the handle and it made a dry squealing sound. This was their only toy, she thought.

When they had reached the centre of the village, Tricia saw two of the dogs which she had been petting earlier. They were mating, stuck end to end, as if someone had tied their tails together. The bitch was smaller than the male dog, her hind legs raised off the ground. Once before, Tricia had seen a pair of boxers which belonged to their neighbours in Hartford, locked together in the same ridiculous position, starting off in opposite directions. Sally had tried to explain to her what it was all about and Tricia had often wondered whether there was any pleasure in the act. They looked so miserable.

As soon as the children caught sight of the mating dogs they began to shout and squeal. Tricia watched in disbelief as they ran towards the dogs with their sticks. They picked up stones and threw them at the dogs, which yelped and tried to get away. But the children had surrounded them and started dancing in a frenzied circle. The male dog dragged the bitch behind him as he searched for some escape. One or two of the children started to beat the dogs with their sticks and Tricia heard their shrieks of delight along with the frantic cries of the dogs.

She was unable to move, paralyzed by the brutality of the children. Covering her face, she screamed for them to stop but they didn't seem to hear. Tricia could do nothing and felt an awful sense of horror and revulsion, staring at the violent knot of dancing children.

A man appeared in the doorway of the last hut and shouted angrily. The children scattered at the sound of his voice, which was vaguely familiar. Tricia was blinded by her tears and did not recognize Gautam until he came towards her. The dogs had disappeared along with the children, making a quick escape.

Tricia covered her face again. The obscenity overpowered her and she felt sick and afraid. There was a weakness in her legs, a clumsy, spastic feeling as if her knees were going to give way. Gautam caught her by the arm.

"How could they be so cruel?" she said.

Silently and without explanation, he led her past the huts and down the hill on the opposite side of Kaproli, facing the stream but out of sight of the clinic. There was a twisted ber tree, beneath which was a level patch of ground, a quiet spot. Gautam seated himself on a flat stone and motioned for Tricia to sit beside him. She was still shaking but relieved to be away from the village, the dogs and children. Gautam seemed to be waiting for her to speak.

"Thank you," she said.

"For what?" said Gautam, in English.

"For stopping them. I thought they were going to kill the dogs," she said.

"They meant no harm," he said.

Gautam took out a packet of cigarettes and choosing one for himself, hesitated and then offered them to her. Tricia shook her head.

His polite gesture puzzled her. It was so unexpected, just like his accent. He spoke English in a quiet, almost courteous manner, though Tricia could still sense his anger.

"Have you taken many photographs?" asked Gautam, pointing at her camera.

Tricia looked down in embarrassment. The camera felt like a heavy weight around her neck, a kind of albatross, she thought.

"Only a few."

"Are they colour pictures?"

"Yes," she said.

"And what will you do with them?" he asked, sarcastically. "Put them in an album?"

"Maybe," she said.

"What kind of pictures do you take?" he asked. "Pictures of starving children? So that you can show people in America what India is really like?"

"They're for myself," she said.

"That camera makes you look like a tourist," he said and turned his face away in disgust.

Tricia stared at Gautam, trying to overcome the feeling of shame and understand his hostility. Whenever she met a person for the first time, she knew that sooner or later they would ask her where she came from. All her life she had been forced to explain, telling people that she was an orphan, that she had come to America when she was just over a year old, that she was born somewhere near a little town in India called Pipra. Ever since she could remember the explanation had annoyed her and sometimes she would refuse to answer, saying, "It's a very long story." She hated to recite the events again and again. People always asked the same dumb questions, "What does it feel like to be an orphan?" The explanations always sounded like an apology, which irritated Tricia even more, as if she were being forced to make excuses for other people's curiosity.

But Gautam was somehow different. For the first time it occured to Tricia that he already knew about her past. He probably knew more of the truth than she herself.

"Why did you come back?" asked Gautam.

"I guess I wanted to find out if there was anything more to know about myself."

"Had you never met Dr Fry before?" said Gautam.

Tricia shook her head.

"Not since I was old enough to remember."

"How do you find him?" said Gautam.

"I think he's wonderful," said Tricia, watching him with caution.

"Oh, he's a good man," said Gautam, but in the way he said it, she could sense a note of disapproval.

"I thought he'd be some kind of holy-roller, converting the heathen," said Tricia. "I never knew what a missionary was like. He seems so kind and generous."

"Of course, but he's a bit of a boy scout, don't you think?" said Gautam.

Tricia laughed, remembering the jack-knife.

"What is it?" said Gautam.

"I was only laughing because that's exactly how I thought of him, as a boy scout," she said. "But I don't think there's anything wrong with that."

"These people need more than Christian charity," said Gautam.

"He saves their lives," said Tricia.

"Sometimes, yes. But to what end?"

"He saved your life," said Tricia.

Now, he laughed.

"Is that what he told you?" said Gautam.

Tricia wished she hadn't said it.

"I have nothing against Dr Fry," said Gautam. "He comes to Kaproli with his car and instruments, his thermometers and bottles of medicine. The villagers flock to him. They are addicted to his pills and his kindness."

"So what?" said Tricia, defensively.

"I only wonder what will happen when he leaves," said Gautam. "They have become dependent on him, these people. Dr Fry is getting old. Maybe he's got another ten years to live at the very most, or else he'll go back to America on retirement. Then where will these people get their medicines?"

"You can't blame him for that," she said.

"A lot of people believe in doing good but it's really nothing more than self-delusion," said Gautam. "It soothes our conscience and nothing else, satisfies our own emotions."

"Dr Fry said you were a communist."

Gautam laughed.

"I wonder what he meant by that," he said.

Gautam paused to crush the butt of his cigarette beneath his chappal.

"I used to be like you. I felt pity for those who suffered," he said, "until I realized that I was being sentimental. Pity is an unnatural thing. Those children, they felt no pity. For you it was an act of cruelty, beating the dogs. To them it was a joke. They found it funny."

"So you think nobody should care if people suffer?" said Tricia. "We should be insensitive?"

"No, that's not what I mean at all," said Gautam. "What I'm trying to say is that we have to look beyond the pain and hunger to the actual cause of suffering. Pity is nothing but a selfish, worthless response."

Tricia was silent for a while, staring down at the dust between her feet.

"Are these people very poor?" she asked, pointing towards the village.

"What does it look like to you?" he said.

"I mean, how do they survive?"

"They live off the forest. They have their goats. They grow a little. Sometimes they work for the forest contractors or on the road gangs. It's always hand to mouth."

"Are they starving?" she said.

This time Gautam looked at her impatiently. Tricia could tell her questions angered him, but she couldn't stop herself, wanting to prod him further and find the core of his bitterness. For a moment she was afraid that he would get up and leave. He seemed to take offence so easily, not just because of something she'd said or done but simply because she was there.

"Yes, they are starving" he said, "but not as you'd imagine. They eat, maybe once a day. The children are malnourished."

"I really don't have any conception of hunger," she said. "Prolonged hunger. Do people actually starve to death?"

"Not at this time of year," said Gautam, coldly, "but if there is a drought or the summer goes on for a few weeks more than it should, the weaker ones die off."

"Doesn't anyone give them food?"

"No," said Gautam. "Sometimes they can get a free meal at the temple in Pipra but that's a long walk, six miles both ways. And during the elections they are given wheat and rice but that's only once in three or four years."

"Can't they farm some more of the land?"

"They have no land," said Gautam. "They are tribals. All of this belongs to the forest department and they are only permitted to have their huts. Those fields by the stream are illegal, their goats are illegal. They have to bribe the forest guards to cut fodder and firewood."

"Do they hunt?" she asked.

"Yes, sometimes, but there's not much game left in the forest and they are lucky if they get a hare or a hornbill."

"It is so depressing," she said, "I can't help it. Sometimes I just don't want to look, like with the dogs."

Gautam glared at her.

"You could always go back to America," he said, "and forget that you have ever been to Pipra."

His voice took on a bitter timbre of disdain. In a strange way, she wanted him to shout at her, to abuse her innocence and naïvity.

"Does it disgust you, this poverty?" said Gautam.

"No," said Tricia, shaking her head.

"Then why are you afraid to look, because you are ashamed?" he said. "What is it that makes you turn away? The memory of a happy childhood?"

Tricia could feel the children surrounding her and hear their shouts and cries. She was sitting absolutely still, with her knees drawn up to her chin. She was not crying, but had her eyes closed, imagining the pelting stones, the sharp sticks coming down on top of her and the high-pitched, gleeful laughter of the children. Tricia bit her lips to keep from screaming.

Gautam got to his feet. He did not say goodbye, but tossed his cigarette away and turned to leave. She wanted to call after him and ask him more, but she was afraid. It was as if Gautam had touched a nerve but instead of pain, there was a numbed sensation. Tricia watched him climb back up the hill and disappear into the village.

TWO

THERE IS a legend amongst the tribals of Pipra that the goddess was born from an egg made of clay, which had been fashioned by an aged potter, who lived alone in a hut on the bank of the river Ladhya. The potter worked a whole year to create the egg, gathering the best clay from the river bottom and forming it carefully on his wheel. He smoothed it lovingly with his fingers, painted designs on the shell and left it to bake in the sun. The old potter intended to give the egg as an offering to God. But one evening, when he came to see if it was hardened, he found that the egg had been shattered. Standing nearby was a woman dressed in simple clothes. The potter thought that the woman had broken the egg and he cursed her, saying that her children would live in hunger, as animals of the forest, naked, scavenging for food. Terrified by the old man's words, the goddess revealed herself and explained to the potter that she had been hatched out of the egg, pleading with him to renounce the curse. The potter was full of remorse but there was nothing he could do. His words had already been uttered. The goddess had two sons who ruled as kings of Pipra for thirty years but eventually the curse came true. The kingdom was invaded and they were forced to take refuge in the jungle, living off roots and berries.

Gautam tried to imagine the giant terracotta egg incubating on the river bank. He had heard the story many times, usually sung to the accompaniment of a crude thumb piano. The music was plaintive and had a haunting quality. The tune repeated itself over and over in his mind but he could not remember the words of the refrain.

At one time, the story used to make him angry. He couldn't understand why the tribals still believed in a curse which was uttered hundreds of years ago. To Gautam's mind it was a facile apology for the humiliation and suffering of the tribals, an illogical superstition, a false myth, a distortion of history. There were other stories about the goddess as well, songs of penance and devotion. But when the tribals gathered at night in the forest, around their cooking fires, within the mud walls of their huts, it was this song which was sung most of all and seemed to touch the core of their disillusionment.

The shrill ululation of the singers had a mournful sound, almost bird-like. Listening to them, it seemed to Gautam as if only a few days or weeks had passed since the tribals were exiled from their kingdom, not centuries. Their shadows swayed in the firelight. As he tried to remember the words of the refrain, Gautam realized that he had almost come to believe in the curse himself. The tune of the song seemed to taunt him until finally the words fell into place with the music:

> *I broke the shell of my earthen womb,*
> *Thrown on the wheel, and baked in the sun,*
> *Born to the curse of the potter's tongue.*

Upstream from Kaproli there was a disused trail which zig-zagged through the jungle of lantana. Gautam followed it, using a stick to break the spider webs that came in his way and brushing aside the thorns and branches which had grown across the path. Several weeks had gone by since the rains had ended and the stream was hardly a trickle now, flowing amongst the rocks and sand-bars. The water was a metallic green in the dusty sunlight. On the opposite bank a pair of lapwings were calling, a shrill, accusing cry. Gautam found that the tune of the song was no longer on his mind, now that he remembered the words.

Several years ago a team of archæologists had come to Pipra. Gautam met them briefly at their dig, a barren mound on the outskirts of town. They came from Delhi University and were searching for a mediæval ruin mentioned in the journals of a Turkish traveller from the twelfth century. Their search was unsuccessful and when Gautam met them they were packing up to leave. The team had excavated to a depth of about forty feet, scraping off layer upon layer of soil. The archæologist who showed Gautam around the dig told him that they had been hoping to find the foundations of a palace which was supposed to have been built of jade and marble but they had obviously been misled in their research. All that they had unearthed were quantities of potsherds. The archæologist had pointed to one embedded in the wall of earth. He dug the piece of terracotta out with his fingers and showed it to Gautam. The potsherd was brittle, with sharp edges and slightly rounded, not unlike a fragment of a giant eggshell . . . .

Gautam was disturbed by his conversation with Tricia and regretted having been abrupt with her, not because of what he'd said but out of a feeling that he had exposed himself. There was something disquieting about Tricia, a kind of unpredictable innocence. As a boy, he had been jealous of her, wishing that he could escape from Pipra, from the claustrophobia of the mission compound, from his parents, from the stigma of Christianity. He had often imagined Tricia in America, living in a Christmas-card house, surrounded by snow and ice, opening package after package full of mechanical toys and chocolates wrapped in cellophane – the glossy, cheerful world of fireplaces and Christmas bells. It seemed so different and so distant from the compound and the forest.

Ahead of him, he could see the low hut which stood by itself in a clearing next to the stream. It looked deserted, except for the whiskers of smoke which curled from under the roof. Two dogs were lying in the sun. They lifted their heads but did not bark. The hut stood all by itself, not far from the stream and in the shade of a tall amla tree. A pair of goats had climbed onto the roof of the hut and were chewing at the thatch. A woman came out of the hut and shouted at the goats, throwing a stick at them, so that they leapt down and ran away. She was about to go back inside again, when she noticed Gautam and stopped. Instead of greeting him, she glanced up at the roof again.

"If I didn't watch them every minute, they'd surely eat the roof from over my head." She paused. "Do you have a cigarette?"

Gautam said nothing, but reached into the pocket of his shirt and took out a packet, from which he offered her one. He gave her a box of matches as well and watched her light the cigarette.

"I haven't seen you for a long time," she said, "I thought you might have run away from Pipra."

Gautam shook his head and smiled. She had a way of speaking, that always made him feel as though he was still a child, even though she was only four or five years older than him. Her clothes were simple, but clean. She wore a scarf over her hair and she was barefoot. Unlike most tribal women she didn't wear much jewelry, only an ivory bracelet on her arm and a silver amulet. She was still a beautiful woman, with a strength in her limbs that gave her a graceful appearance, even though her hands and feet were cracked and gnarled from caring for the goats. Gautam could remember those hands when there were smooth and delicate, with tapered wrists and agile fingers. He remembered how she would sit with her daughter asleep in her lap and tell about the forest beyond the hills. No matter how old she grew, Gautam would always think of Mamta as the girl he'd known on the compound, his playmate and friend.

The hut had once belonged to a man named Shetru. He had made a living by working as a labourer for the forest department and sometimes gathering herbs and wild honey in the forest. Shetru had come to the hospital for treatment while Mamta was still living on the compound. He suffered from ulcers and almost died of bleeding. Mamta had known him from before, when he had worked with her father, long ago, cutting trees for a timber contractor. She recognized him one day at the hospital and used to take him food while he was sick.

Gautam had learned all this from one of the sweepers at the hospital and from the villagers of Kaproli. Shetru had been an unpleasant man, without friends or family. He liked to keep to himself and had his hut some distance from the village. Gautam had never really understood what happened, but when Mamta ran away from the compound, she came to live with Shetru. Less than a year later, Shetru got drunk in town and was run over by a truck. The villagers had assumed that Mamta would go back to her own village or to the compound after Shetru died. One or two had offered to buy the goats from her, but she stayed on, tended her flock, grew a few vegetables and lived by herself in the forest. She had learned that she could rely on no one but herself.

Inevitably the rumours started and sympathies changed. The men began to visit her. One or two of the self-righteous villagers called her a whore. Most of them mentioned it with a touch of embarrassment. But they did not mistreat her and since she lived apart already there was no question of ostracizing Mamta. She had acquired a reputation as a dependable midwife and the villagers called her in for difficult deliveries. Mamta kept a biscuit tin – Gautam remembered it had come from Miss Reynolds's kitchen – full of potions and herbs. She never sat and talked with the other women of Kaproli, except on special occasions, a wedding, a celebration. She kept herself aloof, knowing better than to expect too much kindness. For her, each act seemed to be a simple transaction – selling the goat kids, copulating with the men, delivering the children. Only the tribal men visited her. She lived too far from Pipra for anyone from town to walk the distance.

When Gautam returned to Pipra after leaving college, he was determined to find out what had happened to Mamta. Nobody in Pipra had seen her for almost fifteen years. Gautam's work at the hospital took him to all the villages around and with the help of the hospital sweeper who remembered Shetru, he finally found her hut above Kaproli.

Mamta was gathering beanpods from under a tree when he saw her first and he recognized her immediately. Gautam greeted her and she looked at him suspiciously, asking him how he knew her name. By then he'd grown his beard and for awhile she did not believe that it was him. Their first meeting had been awkward and she seemed reserved, unwilling to talk about herself, suspicious of his motives.

"Are you a doctor?" she asked, when he told her that he was working at the hospital.

"No, I'm a social worker," he said.

"What is that?" asked Mamta.

"I go around the villages and visit patients once they leave the hospital, to make sure that they are taking their medicines, things like that," he said.

"You try to turn them into Christians?" she said, sarcastically.

"No," he said, shaking his head. "How could I, when I am no longer a Christian myself?"

She seemed surprised.

"I thought that you would become a padre like your father," said Mamta.

After that, he visited her whenever he went to Kaproli and Mamta became more friendly. They talked together for hours about his childhood, her brief marriage to Shetru, his experiences at college. Mamta was frank and open about the way she lived and supported herself. The only thing she would never talk about was her daughter and the reason why she had left the compound. Gautam had tried to ask her once but she had taken his hand and put it over his mouth, as if to silence him. He could tell that she did not want to speak about these things as if it were an evil secret which could not be mentioned for fear of retribution.

After he had visited Mamta several times, she asked him openly whether he wanted to make love with her, except she used a word from her own dialect which he didn't understand and for a moment Gautam thought she wanted a cigarette, she said it so casually.

They were sitting in her hut and Mamta had given him a glass of tea. Laughing at his embarrassment, she stood up and took him by the hand. She led him to the low, rope cot which stood in one corner of the hut, covered with a cotton mattress. Mamta lay down on her back and drew her skirt above her waist. He felt as though she was making him do it, as if she meant to defile him, to erase all that there had been between them, almost as a revenge against the hypocrisy of the compound. It was not an act of love, but something desperate and full of pain. Gautam took her quickly, without thinking, without holding back. As a boy he had imagined making love to Mamta and those first dreams of love had always been so gentle, so coy and unexpected. He had never felt guilty, picturing Mamta in this way. But now, years later, he thrust himself on her without any of that love, as if forcing himself against her will. As he struggled inside of her, Gautam could hear the grating howl of the dust storm, doors clapping in the wind, the crackle and boom of thunder. He saw the child imprisoned in the bottle, a bestial vision, the wrinkled hands and feet, two tiny bodies fused together. Gautam buried his face in Mamta's throat to stifle his cries and she too fought with him, her arms gripped about his waist, their legs entangled and the rhythm of their bodies, agitated not by passion but by a desperate need. The child seemed to grow larger, pressing against the sides of the bottle. Gautam clamped his eyes tightly shut but the child continued to expand until the bottle shattered. Gautam screamed as if his lungs had burst.

Afterwards, he felt a sense of shame and disgust. When he tried to give her money, Mamta turned her face away and shook her head. Gautam did not spend the night, but returned to Kaproli where he went down to the stream and bathed, rubbing his skin with sand, trying to rid himself of her smell, the rich, offensive odour of goats.

Gautam never slept with Mamta again. When he was in the area he would occasionally stop to have a cigarette with her and share the village gossip. But that was all. Once, he saw her leaving Kaproli after she had helped at the birth of a child, carrying the biscuit tin and a young chicken which had been given to her as payment. It was early dawn and a cold morning. Mamta looked like a visiting spirit leaving with the night.

As he ducked down and entered the hut, Gautam could smell the bitter-sweet odour of liquor. Mamta had a makeshift still erected over the hearth – a blackened tin cannister on top of which there was a brass water vessel, the base of which was fitted into the cannister. From one side, a plastic pipe emerged and a clear, yellowish liquor was dripping into a smokey bottle. Mamta had learned her brewing skills from Shetru and she sold the drink to village men who came to visit her. There were some people who said she had more money than anyone else in Kaproli and kept it hidden in a buried pot under the floor of her hut. Mamta never went to town but some of the men would bring her cakes of raw sugar which she fermented, using special roots and herbs. Gautam had noticed that she never drank herself.

"Do you want to drink?" she asked.

Gautam shook his head. He was wondering how she would react to the news he had to tell her.

"Mamta," he said, "the girl is back."

"Which girl?" she asked, adjusting the sticks in the fire.

"Your daughter," said Gautam. "She's come back to Pipra."

Mamta looked at him, as though her eyes were still adjusting to the darkness of the hut. Crouched beside the fire, she looked much older.

"Have you seen her?" asked Mamta.

"Yes," said Gautam. "She was at Kaproli this morning."

"Why didn't you bring her here to see me?" said Mamta.

"I wasn't sure," said Gautam.

One of the goats had come inside and was gnawing at the ropes on the bed. Mamta shooed it away.

"She must be ten or twelve by now," said Mamta.

"Older than that," said Gautam.

"Is she beautiful?" asked Mamta.

Gautam nodded.

She adjusted her water vessel on the still, using an old rag to seal the edges where the steam was leaking out. The alcohol had a sickly smell, mixed with the stench of goats.

"Why has she come back?" said Mamta, almost to herself.

"She has brought Miss Reynolds's ashes," said Gautam. "For burial."

"The Miss-sahib. I didn't know that she had died."

"Yes, she wanted her ashes to be buried in Pipra," said Gautam.

"Do Christians burn their dead?" said Mamta. "I thought they let them rot beneath the ground."

"It can be either way," said Gautam.

"Why would she want to be buried here?"

"Maybe she liked the place," said Gautam.

Mamta laughed.

"What is it?"

"I was just remembering the Miss-sahib, how she used to hate the dirt and dust of Pipra. She used to make the sweepers mop the floors four times a day and now she herself will become a part of that dirt."

Mamta seemed distracted, as though she had not taken in the fact that Tricia had returned. The goat climbed back onto the bed but this time she ignored it.

"Did you speak to her about me?" said Mamta.

"No," said Gautam. "I'm not sure how much she has been told."

"What would she think of this hut?" said Mamta.

"She speaks no Hindustani," said Gautam.

"Then you will have to translate," said Mamta. She stopped and looked at him. "Do you think the sahib will let her come to see me?"

"Of course," said Gautam. "She is not a child."

He noticed a peculiar expression cross Mamta's face, a look of eagerness and sorrow, as though she could not wait to see the girl and yet she knew that it would bring her sadness as well as joy.

THREE

THE NEXT DAY was Sunday. For almost ten minutes the church bell had been ringing, a steady, persistent sound. Tricia and Dr Fry came out of the bungalow. He was wearing a creased pair of seersucker trousers, a white shirt and tie. His hair was combed and parted which made him look a little older. Tricia had on a beige dress, which she had packed at the last minute, never expecting to have to wear it. They made a curious pair, dressed for church and stepping out from under the thatch. Tricia looked very small beside him, fine-boned and agile. Dr Fry had a lumbering appearance, a look of rough-hewn dignity.

Tricia hadn't gone to church for years, not since she'd started high school. The people of the compound had organized a tea party for her after the service. They wanted to welcome her back to Pipra.

Fry and Tricia took a shortcut through a hole in the hedge, crossed a ditch and went around behind the church. The bell stopped ringing all at once and in the hush she could hear parakeets squabbling. They climbed the steps and entered through the portico. There were about thirty people inside, filling the first six pews. The church could have held four times their number. The men and women were segregated on either side of the aisle. Several people turned and looked back expectantly. Tricia took hold of Dr Fry's arm but one of the women slid over and beckoned for her to sit down. Tricia hesitated, then took her seat and Fry sat down across from her.

Padre Massey stood up and shuffled forward to the pulpit. He put on his glasses and began looking through the pages of his Bible. The congregation sat in silence. Tricia heard a few more people coming in. The sounds from outside, a truck on the road, distant voices at the hospital, seemed far removed from the sanctuary of the church. Fritz and Sally were Unitarians and Tricia could remember the warm, well-upholstered church in Hartford with dark oak timbers and an organ that sounded like a celestial orchestra. Tricia had gone to Sunday school in the basement for a while but they were not regular church people and after a time they went only at Christmas and Easter. This church was different, very plain. There was a simple cross on the wall behind the pulpit, no stained glass windows or tapestries. On one wall was a wooden frame with the hymn numbers. There was a low communion table with a vase of plastic lilies. The church seemed to have been built around the same time as Fry's bungalow. There were fans hanging from the vaulted ceilings. The bare interior of the church, the vaporous clouds of sunlight which entered through the frosted windows, the saturated heat gave Tricia a feeling of emptiness and abandonment.

Leaning on the pulpit, Padre Massey had begun to pray, his eyes closed. Everyone had bowed their heads and Tricia too ducked down self-consciously. The women had their heads shrouded with their saris. The men sat on the other side, holding steepled fingers to their lips. The reverent silence seemed to absorb the pastor's words. Even the children remained in their places without fidgeting. Some of the younger ones sat with the women but the others, wearing their best clothes, oiled hair plastered down behind their ears or braided with ribbons, sat in the front two rows. Padre Massey's voice rose and fell. It was like a chant and Tricia was transfixed by the sound, even though she could not understand the words. Finally, the voice dropped to almost a whisper and the congregation replied in unison, "Amen". It sounded like a complaint. There were so few of them, but the walls of the church had a resonance which amplified their voices.

A young man, whom Tricia had seen in passing at the hospital, began to play a harmonium. He sat on the floor, working the bellows with one hand and picking out the tune with the other. The music had a wheezing sound but the melody was strident. The congregation stood up as the pastor lifted his hands. The hymn sounded vaguely familiar to Tricia. The woman beside her held the hymnal so that both of them could read, but it was all in Hindustani. Tricia stood and listened. The woman had a pleasant voice but most of the congregation was off-key. She could hear Dr Fry as well, a rough baritone. He was so much taller than everyone else, like some kind of giant. The congregation struggled through six verses of the hymn; each time the chorus seemed to get a little louder and the harmonium more shrill.

Padre Massey wore a loose white cassock. He was a frail man with a bewildered expression. He began to speak in English and Tricia realized that he was looking straight at her. Because of his thick accent, it took a moment for her to understand that he was welcoming her on behalf of the congregation. He kept repeating the phrase, "our sweet daughter". The whole congregation had swivelled around in their pews to look at her. Tricia wanted to crawl out of sight. She bowed her head and bit her lip to keep from crying. It was difficult for her to believe that they remembered her. They had been waiting for her all this time, their "sweet daughter". Soon the pastor ran out of words and opened the Bible to read the lesson.

There was another hymn and then a rambling sermon in which Padre Massey looked at Tricia meaningfully several times. Two children in the pew ahead of her had turned around and were kneeling, facing Tricia. She tried to smile at them but they only stared as though she were some kind of oddity. The collection was taken up. They sang another hymn and the pastor gave the benediction.

The woman next to Tricia took her by the hand and stood up. They smiled at each other. The congregation started to filter out of the church. The woman wouldn't let go of Tricia's hand as they went down the aisle. Dr Fry had been cornered by two men in suits. He glanced at her but by now the other women had surrounded Tricia and were leading her away. She felt as though she were being abducted. So far, they had not said anything to her. Near the door there was a baptismal font made of marble. It was ornately carved with floral patterns but there was a crack in it. The women guided her to the font and pointed. Tricia was puzzled until a young woman, whom she recognized as a nurse from the hospital spoke in English.

"In this, you were baptized," she said.

Someone had grabbed her other hand as well and she felt the women pressing against her, their well-meaning faces, their earnestness, their curious eyes. It was as though they held some claim on her. Their voices surrounded her. Here and there she caught an English phrase. Tricia stared at the marble basin, wondering how it had cracked. There was no water in it and it was covered with dust, but there was still a lustre to the stone, a deathly white. Tricia once again felt the tears and held them back, distracting herself by staring at the faces of the women. They seemed so eager to touch her. When one released her hand, another took hold of it. She heard them repeating her name but could not understand what they were saying. Her hands were sweating but the women clung to her, as though in desperation, as though they would never let her go.

The tea party had been laid out under a tamarind tree in the garden of the church. Two rickety tables stood next to each other, covered with white cloths. There were dishes of biscuits and sweets. Each household on the compound had brought their contribution. The hospital peons served tea from large porcelain pots. Tricia was brought to the table and served first, her hands released at last from the bird-like clutches of the women. The men kept their distance.

After they had all been served, Fry came over and introduced her to each of the women, one by one. They stood in a cluster and bobbed their heads when their names were called, smiling shyly as Dr Fry made a teasing remark or pretended to forget their names. Then he took her across to the men, who greeted her with courteous respect. Tricia could only say, "Hello," and "Thank you" as they welcomed her. There was an awkwardness to the introductions.

Soon enough the women whisked her away again to a semi-circle of chairs. One of the girls was sent to refill her tea cup and bring her another plateful of sweets. They seemed so eager to please, so anxious that she feel welcome and at home, that she should be loved and love them in return. Tricia tried hard to be friendly with the women, but she felt trapped and wanted only to get away. They kept offering her different things to eat, doughnuts and little pastries filled with raisins and dry cereal, sickly sweet candies and cake. She had to eat it all, afraid that they would be offended. The women watched her as she ate, as she bit into each different sweet or savoury, how she brushed the crumbs from her dress and drank her tea. They kept touching her nervously, as if to make sure that she was real. They asked her questions about America. What do they eat in America? Is it very cold in America? Were her parents well? Had she any brothers and sisters? Did she like India? How long was she going to stay? Tricia replied politely to each but they hardly seemed to care about the answers. It was enough to have her there, to watch her as she chewed and swallowed, to feel the material of her dress. She hadn't eaten this much for days, but they kept bringing more until she had to refuse.

The woman sitting next to her was wearing coloured glass bangles and when she put her hand on Tricia's arm Tricia noticed them and said that they were pretty. One of the girls giggled and without hesitation the woman pulled them off her wrist and gave them to Tricia.

"No, please. I didn't mean . . ." Tricia shook her head.

But the woman insisted. "For you," she said.

"I only said they were pretty," said Tricia, "I didn't ask for them."

But by then the woman had taken her hand and slid the bangles over her wrist. She was insistent.

"You shouldn't," said Tricia, "really, I only said that they were pretty."

Tricia was relieved when it was over. Fry took her back to the bungalow. She went into her room and stood alone for awhile under the fan. The tears streamed down her face and she no longer tried to hold them back.

FOUR

AFTER THE church service and tea party, Dr Fry returned to his office at the hospital. He wanted to catch up on a pile of correspondence which had been lying untended on his desk for more than a week. There was nothing he hated more than paperwork and as he sat down in the old swivelchair which had been at the hospital from before his time, Dr Fry was overcome with a feeling of exhaustion and despair.

Instead of turning his attention to the letters which were stacked on one corner of the desk, Fry reached across to the bookcase and took his Bible from the shelf. It was an old King James with a crocodile cover and flimsy pages, like airmail paper. The Bible had belonged to his wife. Her maiden name was written on the title page, Patricia Sommers, in perfect, flowing copperplate. You could tell that she had been beautiful, just from her handwriting. Patricia had given it to him before leaving on the troopship from Bombay.

It had been a long time since Dr Fry had opened his Bible. Years ago, he used to make a habit of reading a chapter every day but like his other routines, that had fallen through with the growing work load at the hospital. Dr Fry had always enjoyed the Old Testament, the flowery language, the history, the psalms. He was proud of the fact that he could still read the fine print without difficulty, never having worn a pair of glasses in his life.

He opened to a chapter in Isaiah which had always comforted him in its complete surety of salvation, an aged prophet convinced that a messiah would appear. I have never been much of a believer, thought Fry. If someone had told me in high school that I was going to be a missionary, I would have laughed at them. He never had that sort of faith, not the way Patricia did. She was the one who decided that they should come to India.

Once or twice a year some tail-gate evangelist came riding through Pipra and held a prayer meeting at the compound. The wild exhortations and gilded promises always depressed Fry. He much preferred the Sunday worship service with Padre Massey, the plastic flowers, the Roman Urdu, the old hymns sung off-key to the groaning of the harmonium. It was sad in its own way, the broken pews and termites, the geckos climbing the pulpit. But the yellow church was still the sanctuary of his faith, just as the hospital was his workplace and the bungalow his home.

He had never felt comfortable with the idea of conversion. There were those missionaries who believed their only purpose was to proselytize amongst the Indians, to rescue souls for Christ. Fry had always thought of them as trophy hunters. For him, his mission was to be a witness, nothing more, to live a Christian life according to his own conscience, to set an example of selfless commitment and compassion.

Dr Fry was basically a practical man. He believed in the accomplishments of his own two hands. There were mission doctors who put their faith in the powers of the holy spirit, the gift of healing. Fry had always been impatient with their prayers, their laying on of hands and holy water, which seemed to betray a lack of confidence in their own abilities. He believed that prayers should only be offered after the final suture had been sewn. The simple logic of his beliefs helped to ease the sense of futility which seemed to hover over Pipra like a dust haze. Fry had learned to submerge his doubts under a constant burden of work, absorbing himself in the delicate procedures of surgery, the complexities of diagnosis, the endless routines which a hospital requires. The physical exertion of his work as well as the mental concentration which it demanded, masked whatever hopelessness he might have felt in the face of human suffering, the prevalence of pain and disease, the intimate agonies of death.

When his wife, Patricia was killed, Dr Fry had thought of leaving India. He did not believe in the strength of his own commitment. But then, the more he thought of it, the less the idea of returning to a small town practice in Ohio appealled to Fry. It would seem as though his wife had died for nothing. He felt that he would have betrayed her memory by leaving Pipra.

The other missionaries were full of condolences and tried to be understanding. They suggested that he should take a trip up to the mountains, get away to Kashmir for awhile. But Fry had realized that the only way he could survive was by absorbing himself entirely in his work. After the first long evening which he spent alone, reading and re-reading the letter from the American consulate in Bombay, telling of Patricia's death, sitting motionless under the whirling fan, wishing somehow that he had been taken into the army, despite his knee, to go racing up a beach into the stuttering murder of the Japanese guns; after that he knew that there was nothing worse than idleness. His work at the hospital became an obsession and he began to push himself beyond the normal limits of endurance, in an effort to forget, to absolve those memories. He knew that if he stopped for even a second, the shadows of despair and hopelessness would converge on him.

For years now, he had lived that way. The work was a kind of renunciation, a form of escape. Fry immersed himself in the practical routines and duties the way an ascetic absorbs himself in meditation. As the years went on, it helped him to forget not only the death of his wife but the prospect of retirement. What he feared now more than anything else, was the idea of being unable to work, of being forced into a life of endless leisure.

There were times, of course, when he had stopped himself and wondered at his own asceticism. He was aware of the loneliness which he kept at arms length, the moments of exhaustion, the sleepless nights in which he tried to read and couldn't concentrate. It was a kind of boredom, a gnawing feeling of frustration which drove him back to work. Sometimes he would rise at two or three in the morning and go across to the hospital and surprise the nurses on duty with a sudden, ghostly appearance. There was always something to be done, a patient who needed to be cared for, a microscope which didn't work, or the X-ray machine which was always going on the blink. Even at the oddest hours of the night, he would find something to occupy his time.

Dr Fry had always wanted children and he could still remember the excitement which he'd felt when his wife had told him that she was pregnant. They had not expected to be parents quite so soon, but everything seemed to be happening at once. And then a few months later, when Patricia had to leave for America, he had been disappointed that he would not be with her for the birth. There had been so much to hope for in the future and it had vanished all at once.

The thought of adopting a child had never really occured to Fry, but years afterwards, when Mamta abandoned the girl, it seemed the most natural thing for him to do, taking the baby into his home, as if he had fulfilled some lost desire. For a brief year Dr Fry had been very happy and he was always eager to go back to the bungalow and see the girl. The large rooms did not seem so empty any more and even when the baby cried it made him happy, for he was no longer by himself. He felt a renewed sense of hope and optimism, as though he had been cleansed. He no longer felt the need to drive himself to the point of exhaustion, before he could fall asleep.

Dr Fry riffled the pages of his Bible in a gesture of regret, remembering the unrestrained joy of those few months of fatherhood, the freedom and delight which he had never known before. And now, as he sat there in his office, an older man, he realized how tenuous those hopes had been, how fragile, how easily shattered and destroyed.

Tricia's legs ached. She wasn't used to exercise, but she persisted, refusing to give up. Her face was dripping with sweat and her shirt was plastered to her back. The seat was uncomfortable and she could feel it chafing her legs, as her knees moved up and down like pistons, her breath catching in her throat. Tricia tried to keep a steady rhythm, pacing herself. The bamboo frame was squealing softly at the joints. The chugging of the pump sounded as if there were some dangerous creature in pursuit, breathing down her neck.

She had learned how to ride a bicycle soon after the Crawfords moved to Hartford. For her seventh birthday, Fritz and Sally bought her a bright yellow Schwinn with trainer wheels. Tricia could still remember the first time she rode the bicycle, Fritz holding the carrier, wheels wobbling, her feet slipping off the pedals. She forgot to use the brake and ploughed straight into the neighbour's forsythia, hearing Fritz shouting instructions as she lost control. Tricia had never been very good at keeping her balance and Fritz and Sally didn't trust her enough to let her bike to school, even when she was older.

Tricia glanced over her shoulder and saw that the girl was awake. All she could see were the large, dark, eyes and the tangled strands of hair on the pillow. Tricia leaned forward again, staring at the brick wall in front of her, crouched over the handlebars. She felt as though she was travelling over an endless road, without landmarks, a perpetual journey into nowhere. Her blood was pumping in time with the motion of her legs and she could feel a vein in her temple pulsating gently. She gripped the handles of the bicycle with determination, refusing to stop, caught up in the relentless momentum of the machine.

Tricia had come across to the hospital around eleven o'clock, a short while after the tea party at the church. She felt a brittle tension within herself, a feeling of uncertainty and frustration.

The girl had been asleep when Tricia arrived. One of the hospital peons was taking a turn on the iron lung, pedalling without much effort, as though he were going for a leisurely ride, in no particular hurry. Tricia stood quietly beside the bed. The girl still had the tube in her throat. Dr Fry had said he thought she was improving, though it was too early to tell how badly her body would be affected. One of the valves on the pump had stopped working and he had spent an hour repairing it, early that morning before they'd gone to church.

Tricia stood beside the girl for several minutes, then touched the peon's sleeve, gesturing for him to get down from the bicycle. He hesitated but Tricia pointed to herself insistently, not making a sound for fear of waking the girl. Finally the man dismounted. Just as Tricia climbed onto the seat, Sister Tara came in and waved for her to stop. Tricia smiled and shook her head. The pedals were a lot stiffer than she had expected and at first she thought her legs might not be strong enough, but gradually the bicycle came to life. There was a peculiar feeling of movement, even though the machine was stationary.

Tricia could remember riding her bicycle around the neighbourhood in Hartford. Their house was on a quiet street called Adams Lane and there was a hill at the end, where it merged with Chestnut Street. During the day there were hardly any cars and she would ride her yellow Schwinn up and down the hill. The trainer wheels had been taken off shortly after Tricia got the bicycle and she had fallen several times and scraped her shins and knees. Sally had told her that if she kept on doing that, she'd never be able to wear skirts when she grew up. It all came back to her in a whirl of memories, the bicycle, the streets, the happy suburban childhood, the crew-cut lawns. Up and down the lane she went, the rubber tires sucking at the asphalt. One time she'd tried to go in circles, round and round, turning the steering a little more sharply each time, until she became dizzy and the front wheel locked, sending her flying over the handlebars, skinning her knees, a feeling of weightlessness, the street tilting upwards to the sky – the vertigo, as if the houses were upside down.

"Patricia."

She heard her name and glanced around. Gautam was standing there with his hands in his pockets, studying her.

"Hello," she said, still pedalling.

"The nurse wants you to stop," he said. "They're going to bathe the girl."

Tricia nodded and lifted her feet free of the pedals, which kept turning on their own. She swung her leg over the cross-bar of the bicycle and got down. Sister Tara was standing by with a jug of warm water and towels and one of the peons had brought a basin and a screen.

Gautam stared at the girl in the iron lung, with a serious, thoughtful look on his face.

"How is she now?" he asked.

"Dr Fry says that she's improving," said Tricia. "Another day or two and she won't be needing this. She'll be able to breath on her own."

They walked slowly to the end of the ward where Tricia stopped under a fan to cool herself.

"Did you come here to see Dr Fry?" she said.

"No," said Gautam, "I wanted to speak with you."

Tricia was surprised by this.

"What for?" she said. "Do you think I need another lesson in poverty?"

Gautam shook his head and frowned.

"I came to tell you that I know where your mother lives," said Gautam.

He spoke quite softly but the words seemed to echo within the silence of the hospital.

"My mother," said Tricia. "Where?"

"She lives in the forest, not far from where we were just yesterday."

"Does she know I'm here?" said Tricia.

"Yes, I've told her," said Gautam.

Tricia looked at him and shook her head, confused.

"Why didn't you tell me this before?" she said.

"I thought that you might not want to see her. I thought you might hate your mother because she abandoned you."

"How could I hate someone I never knew?" said Tricia.

As they were standing there, two nurses came by and stared at them. Tricia noticed that they looked at Gautam with obvious expressions of disgust. He ignored them.

"How did you find her?" said Tricia.

"I knew your mother from when I was a boy and later, when I came back after college, I discovered where she was living," he said.

"Did she ever tell you why she ran away and left me?" said Tricia.

"She never talks about what happened," he said. "I think she is quite bitter about it all."

"Bitter?" said Tricia. "Why?"

Gautam looked at her with a puzzled expression.

"Hasn't anyone told you what happened?" said Gautam.

"No," said Tricia.

"Your mother was raped," said Gautam. "That was why she left."

Tricia kept her eyes on him, trying not to let her feelings show.

"Is that really true?" said Tricia.

"Yes, I was here on the compound. I remember when it happened," said Gautam.

"Who was the man who raped her?" said Tricia.

"He was the X-ray technician at the hospital, the son of the woman whom you and your mother were living with."

Tricia was quiet for a moment. The air from the fan was sucking at her clothes and suddenly she felt very cold.

"Why didn't anyone tell me this?" said Tricia.

"They must have been ashamed," he said. "Because he was a Christian they would have kept it quiet."

"Will you take me to see my mother?" asked Tricia.

"Yes," said Gautam.

"When?" said Tricia.

"Tomorrow, around noon there is a bus which will take us part way there. We'll have to walk for several hours."

"That's fine," said Tricia.

"I'll meet you in front of the compound gate at twelve o'clock."

"Yes, I'll be there. Thanks," said Tricia.

Gautam turned abruptly and walked away, but this time instead of the hostility and aloofness which she'd sensed before, Tricia could feel a certain sensitivity in his manner, a feeling of compassion and concern.

For quite a while, Tricia kept standing under the fan. Closing her eyes, she seemed to be spinning around, within a funnel of air. At any moment, it might have lifted her up and swept her away. All along she had suppressed the hope of finding her mother, not wanting to expect the impossible but at the same time imagining herself confronted by this woman she did not recognize and yet who was an image of herself. Sometimes, she had thought of her mother not as a human being but as a gentle creature of the forest, a tree spirit, a bright, transparent figure, slipping through the air without a sound. The breeze from the fan was like the caress of invisible fingers running through her hair. Tricia tried to control the sense of fear and exhilaration which came over her, the shock of knowing that her mother was alive. But with that knowledge there was also the taint of horror and revulsion, having learnt the reason why her mother ran away.

Tricia knocked sharply on the door of Dr Fry's office. She heard him get up from his chair and come across to open the door. Seeing her, he smiled broadly.

"Hello," he said. "Come on in."

The office was cluttered with instruments and papers. Tricia could see that Dr Fry spent very little time in the room. There was an examining table against one wall but it was stacked with files and books. The calendar on the wall was open to the wrong month and there was a musty smell about the room. Fry let her sit down first and then took his seat deliberately, as though she had come in for a consultation. He looked at Tricia with a hesitant smile.

"Is anything wrong?" he said, noticing the serious look in her eyes.

"I was just talking with Gautam," said Tricia. "He says he knows where my mother is living."

"Mamta?" said Fry.

"Yes, and it seems I haven't been told the truth," said Tricia, with a note of impatience in her voice.

Fry waited a moment, as if to catch his breath. He reached across his desk and picked up a paper weight, needing something in his hands.

"Patricia, I know that it must be difficult for you, coming here and learning things you never knew about yourself. That first morning at breakfast you asked me to tell you the whole story. I wasn't sure how much you'd want to hear. Sometimes there are unpleasant things which are best forgotten. I didn't tell you everything about your mother."

"Gautam told me that she was raped," said Tricia.

Fry bowed his head and nodded.

"I want to know what happened," said Tricia. "Please don't try to hide it from me."

Dr Fry turned the paper weight over in his hand. It was made of green glass and there was a chip in it where he had dropped it once.

"Yes, it's true that Mamta was raped and she was beaten up quite badly." He stopped to clear his throat. "I happened to be on duty when they brought her to the hospital. All of the lights were off because of a dust storm which had knocked down the electric lines. Mamta was conscious but in a state of shock. We carried her into this room and at first I didn't realize what had happened. I thought that she'd been injured in the storm. Quite a few trees had fallen down and some of the houses on the compound had been damaged. There was a gash on her forehead and several abrasions on her arms and legs. Her clothes were torn and it was only when the nurses began to take them off, I realized that she'd been raped. It's not a pleasant thing to talk about but I have to tell you everything so that you will understand."

Dr Fry was quiet for a moment. He thought how much the paperweight looked like a baseball in his hand, an emerald baseball which he would hurl into the air as high as it would go, catching the sunlight as it arched across the sky and finally fell to earth.

"Mamta was bleeding quite a bit and I could tell that she was in a lot of pain, though she didn't make a sound. When I began to examine her, she tried to stop me with her hand. She got very agitated and didn't want to let me touch her. I tried to reassure her and attended to the rest of her injuries while the nurses gave her a sedative. When Mamta finally quieted down, I was able to continue my examination. What I discovered puzzled and alarmed me almost as much as the rape itself, for I found that she had been a virgin."

Tricia looked up at him.

"What do you mean?" she said, in a soft, uncertain voice.

"It meant that you were not her daughter," said Fry.

"But, are you sure?" said Tricia.

"I'm absolutely positive," he said. "It was obvious that Mamta had never had intercourse before and certainly never bore a child."

136

Tricia looked at him with an incredulous expression, absorbing the whole weight of what he'd said. The feeling of anticipation and hope which she had felt only a few minutes ago, seemed to escape in a single breath. Now she was alone again, abandoned.

"Then what about me? Where did I come from?" said Tricia.

"I honestly don't know," said Fry. "Mamta was really in no state for me to ask her questions. I treated her as best I could and we put her to bed in one of the wards. The sedative made her groggy and she seemed to be asleep. I decided not to tell anyone, not until I was able to talk with her myself. All along she had pretended to be your mother and nobody had doubted her, even though she was so young. I tried to think of all the possibilities, whether she could have been your sister or maybe she had found you somewhere, lost or abandoned. As it turned out, I never got an answer. Sometime during the night, she got up from her bed and left the hospital. The chowkidar must have been asleep. Just before dawn, the nurses found that she was no longer in her bed. We looked everywhere for her, but she was gone."

"And you never told anyone?" said Tricia.

Fry shook his head.

"I figured it was best to keep things to myself. Everyone was so shocked by what had happened; I didn't see the point in saying anything, once she'd disappeared."

In some ways, Tricia felt relieved. The thought of actually coming face to face with her mother had frightened her. She had often wondered, when she imagined meeting her mother, whether she would actually be able to turn her back and return to America. How would she have spoken to her mother? Would she kiss her? There were so many contradictory responses, bristling inside of her. Tricia smiled at Fry. He looked so sad and disappointed.

"Gautam said that he would take me to meet her, tomorrow," she said.

"Do you think you still want to go?" he asked.

"Yes," said Tricia. "Yes, I do."

FIVE

THE CROWDED, rattle-trap bus stopped at the turning to Kaproli. Gautam and Tricia got down and waited until the bus had started again, with a cloud of diesel fumes and an asthmatic roar of its engine. From there it was about six miles to Mamta's hut, if they took a short cut through the forest.

Tricia was glad to be away from the compound and the hospital. She realized how little she had seen of Pipra. The bus ride she enjoyed, despite the crush of passengers and the noise of the engine. It was a local bus which connected the nearby villages with Pipra and stopped at every crossroads. Tricia and Gautam had boarded at the gate of the compound and had to stand because there were already too many people jammed into the seats. The whole bus seemed as though it was going to fall apart at any minute. One of the villagers was carrying a chicken in his lap and just as they started up from the hospital, the bird got loose and there was pandemonium as she flapped about. One of the other passengers finally got hold of the chicken and passed her back to the owner. Everyone in the bus treated it as a joke and they were still laughing when Tricia and Gautam got out.

Tricia had resisted the urge to bring her camera, remembering what Gautam had said to her. She was still puzzled by his manner, though he was much more friendly now. As they walked along the rutted track he talked quite freely with her. The tone of resentment was gone from his voice.

"Are you in college?" asked Gautam.

"No," said Tricia, "I just graduated this summer."

"What did you study?"

"Psychology," said Tricia.

Gautam seemed amused.

"What for?" he asked. "Is that what you plan to do as a profession?"

"I don't know," she said.

"Will you become a psychiatrist?" he said.

Tricia laughed.

"No, I don't think so," she said. "Psychology doesn't always mean that you become an analyst. It has to do with other things as well."

"Such as?"

"I don't know. Everything, I guess. Personalities. The way a person's mind works. Mostly, I spent my time studying orphans and their sense of identity. Of course, I had a personal interest in the subject."

"What did you discover?" he said.

"Nothing very conclusive. There are so many opinions."

"Is it true that orphans spend their lives searching for their real parents?" he asked.

"In some ways, yes," said Tricia. "Actually, I read a book quite recently in which the author argued that it wasn't the parents whom an orphan is searching for but a long lost brother or sister."

"Did you learn very much about yourself?" he asked.

"Not really," said Tricia. "Towards the end, I got very disillusioned with psychology. It all became so abstract, so scientific and impersonal."

They had stopped for a minute in the shade of an acacia tree which was covered with weaver bird nests, like tassels of straw hanging from the branches. Gautam paused to light a cigarette.

"Are you nervous about meeting your mother?" he asked.

"Yes, of course," said Tricia. "I'm not exactly sure how I'll react."

"Did you ever think about your father, what sort of man he might have been.?"

"No," said Tricia. "It's odd, but I somehow never tried to picture him. Of course he must have been someone but it was always my mother whom I thought about."

They continued walking along the ox-cart tracks. At the sides of the road there were tufts of high grass and termite castles. Tricia felt awkward talking with Gautam, knowing that Mamta was not her mother after all. She wanted to explain to Gautam what Dr Fry had told her, how Mamta had never given birth to a child. And yet somehow, Tricia felt a need to wait until she met the woman herself before deciding on the truth.

"Tell me about Mamta," said Tricia. "What was she like when you knew her on the compound?"

"She was very young, sixteen or seventeen at the most. I was twelve years old. Even though she lived amongst us for only a few months, Mamta left a deep impression on my mind. While she was living on the compound, I became very attached to her.

"She was good to us, as children," said Gautam. "Always ready to play our games and tell us stories. But there was something more than that, a kind of mysterious and magical side to her. She had a wildness about her which excited us, the way she ran when we were chasing her, graceful as an antelope. Her stories too were full of strange creatures and supernatural powers. For me it was a different world completely, after the colourless compound, the Bible stories which were so dull and boring by comparison, the monotonous voices of our mothers gossiping. I was fascinated by her way of speaking. Mamta would use words from her own dialect, phrases which I had never heard before. There was a wonderful sense of freedom about her, even though she had lived such a desperate life; she was like a wild animal which has never been tamed.

"Mamta was beautiful, even though she had a dark complexion. Her face was sensual and her eyes were large and restless. For a young boy, she was everything a woman could be and I suppose that I was madly in love with her. Perhaps she understood what I was feeling, because she used to tease me. She used to say that she would get me a good Christian wife some day, who'd hit me over the head with a rolling pin. I would shout at her and say that I was never going to get married and Mamta would laugh because I got so angry."

"You must have been very upset when she left," said Tricia.

"Yes, I was," said Gautam. "When she disappeared, I was confused and worried. It made no sense to me. Of course, as children we were never told the truth, but it was obvious what had happened. I always had this feeling that Mamta had been rejected, cast out like a stray animal, unwanted and abused. She had been thrown out of the compound for committing some kind of sin, so terrible that no one was willing to say what it was.

"When I came back to Pipra, after leaving medical college, my first instinct was to search for Mamta, to find where she had gone. I didn't even know whether she was still alive or not. It took at least a year and when I found her she had changed. Mamta lived in the forest and never came to Pipra. You see, after she ran away from the compound, Mamta married a man named Shetru, who was a drunkard. He died a year later and left her nothing but the hut. She

140

had some goats of her own and made a living selling these. Mamta also became a village midwife. I could tell that she had suffered a great deal but when I asked her why she left the compound, Mamta would not answer me. Over the years, I have tried many times to get the story from her, but she ignores my questions."

Tricia tried to picture Mamta but somehow she could not bring an image to her mind, only the name – Mamta, it had a simple sound and yet within that name there seemed to be so many different emotions. Sometimes it seemed to her that it was not a name at all but just the sort of sound that a child might make up to call someone, full of affection and happiness.

"Why did you come back to Pipra?" said Tricia.

"Maybe for the same reason that you have come back, to try and understand something of myself, this town where I was born."

"But you don't want to be a part of the compound, do you?"

"No, I could never be a part of that again, the church, the gossip, all that pettiness."

"It must be very depressing," said Tricia.

"Yes, it is sad. Nothing has changed in the last twenty years. They carry on with their prayers, their hymns, their squabbles. Nothing seems to matter to them, outside the walls of the compound."

As they walked for a way in silence Tricia felt the warmth of the sun through her clothes. On either side of them was forest, the unfamiliar trees, the weaver-bird nests and the termite castles.

"Do you think you'll live in Pipra for the rest of your life?" asked Tricia.

"No, I doubt it" said Gautam. "One day, I'll leave. There is really nothing which keeps me here."

"Where would you go?"

"I'm not sure," said Gautam. "There's a friend of mine from college. He has become a trade unionist in Bihar. He always writes and asks me to come and join him. Perhaps it would be interesting. I have never seen Bihar."

They reached the hut by nightfall. Gautam went in first, stooping at the low doorway. He could see four men seated against one wall. They had been drinking and the still was on the fire. When Mamta saw him, she called out in a loud voice, "Here is our social worker. You see, I am making sure that they take their medicine." One of the men laughed. Mamta was about to say something more, when Tricia entered, looking about uncertainly in the firelight.

She saw the woman behind the fire stand up and come towards her. There was a sour, sweet smell in the hut. Mamta came right up to her and put one hand against her face. Tricia stared back at her with a look of amazement in her eyes. They were about the same height, though Mamta was barefoot. The hand moved from Tricia's face to her hair. Suddenly Mamta turned to Gautam and spoke to him, with a tone of disbelief.

"She wants to know why you have cut your hair," said Gautam.

Tricia smiled and Mamta pretended to slap her playfully across the face. The four men were watching them with curiosity. Taking Tricia by the hand, Mamta led her to the place where she'd been sitting. Gautam sat down opposite the men. Again she spoke to Gautam and he translated.

"She says that this hut is all she has. There are no chairs. You shouldn't mind."

Tricia looked at Mamta and shook her head, to say it didn't matter.

Gautam pointed to the still.

"Mamta makes her own homemade liquor and sells it to these men."

"Tonic," said Mamta, using the English word. There was laughter from the men. Tricia could tell that they were drunk. Mamta lifted a grey looking bottle out of the shadows behind her and taking a shallow leaf cup, she poured a drink for Gautam. He took it from her and drank it down in one swallow.

"Tonic," said Mamta, once again and held the bottle up for Tricia to see.

"Would you like some?" said Gautam.

"I'll try just a little bit," said Tricia.

Mamta poured some of the liquor into another cup. Tricia raised it to her mouth and took a sip. The smell was unpleasant and it had a bitter flavour.

"No. No," said Gautam, "This isn't Scotch. You have to drink it all at once."

Tricia hesitated and rolled her eyes. Then tilting back her head, she poured the liquor into her mouth and swallowed quickly. It did not burn her throat or make her cough but the raw taste made Tricia shiver. Mamta laughed and offered her some more. She shook her head. One of the four villagers said something and she passed the bottle across to him. There was a casualness about it all, that made it seem less crude and coarse.

As Gautam began to speak to one of the men, Tricia felt Mamta's hand touching her knee and looked at her. While the men were talking, the two women sat and stared at each other in silence. Tricia felt a sense of recognition, the shadow of a memory passing across her mind. It was something beyond remembering, a feeling of lingering sadness.

Mamta adjusted some of the sticks in the hearth, keeping the fire low. Without speaking, she removed the bottle which had been filling at the still and put her hand under the pipe which was attached to one side of the cannister. She let the distilled liquor trickle over her fingers for a moment and dipped her hand into the fire. Then she held it up for the men to see. Mamta's hand was burning with a pale blue flame and she looked like some kind of medieval conjurer. In the darkness of the hut the alcohol burned with an eerie brightness. After a moment, Mamta shook her wrist and put it out. She passed the liquor to the men and put another empty bottle beneath the pipe.

"Good stuff," said Gautam.

Tricia felt uneasy. There was something grotesque and mysterious about the blue flame and the burning hand.

One of the drinkers pointed at Tricia and said something in a low voice. Gautam smiled and looked at her.

"They want to know if you have come from Delhi," he said.

But before Tricia could say anything, Mamta waved her hand at the men and spoke in an angry voice, as if she were abusing them. After that they would not look at Tricia.

When the bottle had finished, the men got up to leave. One of them could hardly stand and the other helped him to his feet. Mamta went outside with them for a moment and Tricia could hear their voices as they left. By now it was completely dark. One of the dogs barked and she could hear the goats shuffling about in the straw at the other side of the hut. Gautam sat quietly, staring into the fire.

"Those men are from Kaproli," he said. "One of them had a son and they were celebrating."

Mamta came back in.

"Idiots," she said. "They always drink more than they can afford."

She squatted down and removed the bottle which was filling at the still. This time she did not put her whole hand under the pipe but only her fingers and flicked them towards the fire. There was a sputtering sound.

"That's how she tests the liquor," said Gautam. "Now all the alcohol is finished. It's only water."

Mamta smiled and spoke to Tricia.

"She's telling you that she's a wicked woman," said Gautam.

Tricia shook her head once more, wishing that she could answer her.

"I'm sure that isn't true," said Tricia.

Before Gautam could translate, Mamta spoke again.

"She wants to know if you are married."

"No," said Tricia, smiling at Mamta.

There was another exchange between them and Tricia could tell that Gautam did not want to translate what Mamta had said.

"What is it?" said Tricia.

Gautam seemed annoyed.

"She was suggesting that I should marry you," he said.

"Tell her that it wouldn't work. We'd never get along."

Mamta laughed at this.

"She says that you and I can live on the compound. You can work at the hospital," said Gautam.

"Of course," said Tricia. "The only problem is I'm leaving in another week."

"Back to America?" said Gautam.

"Yes, my father's birthday is on the first of October. He's going to be sixty this year. I promised I'd be back for that."

Mamta listened carefully.

"She wants to know what your parents are like," said Gautam.

"Well," said Tricia. "They're an ordinary suburban couple. My father works in a bank and my mother is a housewife. They have their problems."

She waited as Gautam explained to Mamta what she had said.

"Mamta wants to know if you love your parents," said Gautam.

Tricia hesitated and then nodded her head.

"Yes, I do," she said.

"Are your parents very rich?" asked Mamta.

Tricia laughed when Gautam translated this for her.

"I guess they are," she said. "I never thought they were but yes;

144

they have a lot of money."

"And they have no other children?"

"No," said Tricia.

"So you will inherit everything of theirs?" said Mamta.

Tricia felt awkward answering these questions but it seemed very important to Mamta that she should know these things. She asked about the school where Tricia had studied, her clothes, how much it had cost for her to fly to India, the price of milk in America. It all seemed so irrelevant to Tricia and yet she could sense that Mamta was trying hard to understand the kind of life she lived, the conditions under which she had been raised.

As she asked these questions, Mamta removed the still from the fire and put a cooking pot in its place. She made some rice, measuring it out in handfuls into the pot. When she had added some sticks to the fire and brought the rice to a boil, Mamta got up from her place and went to the far side of the hut. Tricia watched her moving about in the shadows and after a moment heard the squawking of a chicken and saw that Mamta had taken a rooster out of the hen coop at the corner of the hut. Before Tricia realized what was happening, Mamta had taken the rooster outside, holding it by both wings.

"Is she going to kill it?" said Tricia, looking at Gautam anxiously.

"Yes," he said. "For our dinner."

"No. She shouldn't. Tell her not to," said Tricia.

"But it's for you," said Gautam.

"I don't want her to," said Tricia. "Please."

Just then, they heard the rooster cry out again, a frantic crowing sound, followed by silence. Tricia knew it was over. The killing had happened out of sight but she felt responsible and frustrated because it had been done for her. Now all at once she was upset by the crude simplicity of Mamta's hut, the smoking fire, the blackened pots, the smell of goats. There was something coarse and unpleasant about it all and yet she did not want to feel that way. She did not want look at it like that and be upset. She wanted to accept Mamta as she was.

A few minutes later, Mamta came back inside carrying the dead rooster. She had plucked most of the feathers and the body looked quite small and naked, the head and feet removed. Tricia thought of the chickens which they bought in the supermarket back home, so frozen and sterile. The sight of those had never upset her but this was different. She could see a few drops of blood on Mamta's skirt.

Mamta sat down at her place by the fire and quickly chopped some onions and then cut the rooster into pieces, working swiftly and speaking from time to time, looking at Tricia and smiling as though nothing had happened. Gautam could tell that Tricia was upset and he tried to distract her, but she watched Mamta making their dinner and gradually her disgust and horror faded.

"Mamta says that she hopes you will not mind the simple food. This is all she has. If she had known that you were coming she would have been prepared," said Gautam.

Tricia nodded and said nothing, wishing that she could speak to Mamta herself.

It was quite late when everything was finally cooked and Mamta took two enamel plates from a box near the fire. She wiped these clean and served the rice and chicken with a large steel spoon. When the plate was put in front of her, Tricia looked down at it with a helpless expression.

"Have you ever eaten with your fingers?" said Gautam.

Tricia shook her head.

Gautam said something to Mamta. She turned and hunted through the box and finally produced a spoon with a dented handle. Wiping it on the corner of her skirt, she gave it to Tricia. Gautam had already begun to eat, shovelling the rice and chicken into his mouth with his fingers. Tricia held the spoon but she could not bring herself to take a bite. She could not get over the thought of the rooster being killed and the sound of its cries. Tricia felt ashamed. She did not want to offend Mamta by not eating and yet the mound of rice and the sight of the chicken pieces on her plate made her lose all appetite.

Mamta seemed to understand. She was not eating herself and shifted closer to Tricia, taking the plate in her lap. With her right hand she picked up the wing of the chicken and tore off a piece of the flesh. Then she lifted her hand to Tricia's mouth, for her to eat. Tricia took the bite, expecting to gag on it, tasting the spices and the sweet flavour of the meat. She chewed and swallowed. Mamta had now taken some of the rice as well and squeezing it together deftly with her fingers, she gave her another mouthful. Tricia did not resist, even though she still felt some hesitation at the thought of what it was that she was eating. They said nothing and after awhile it seemed quite normal to have Mamta feeding her and Tricia was no longer disturbed by the killing of the rooster. She could tell that Gautam was watching but she did not care. There was a gentleness about the way that Mamta fed her which made her feel secure and safe. The darkness of the hut, the smoke, the goat smell did not bother her any more. Mamta continued to feed her until the plate was empty and Tricia ate as if she were a hungry child.

During the meal they had not spoken and afterwards there was a long silence. Mamta poured another drink for Gautam.

"Why is she not eating?" asked Tricia.

Gautam asked the question.

"She will eat later," he said, after Mamta answered.

The glow from the fire lit their faces and outside there were night sounds, crickets and the far off barking of a dog.

"Please tell her that Dr Fry has explained everything to me," said Tricia.

Gautam translated and after he had finished, Mamta looked at her with a pensive expression. Without taking her eyes off Tricia she said something to Gautam.

"She wants to know what he has told you," said Gautam.

"Dr Fry says that I am not her daughter." said Tricia.

Gautam looked at her with disbelief.

"Is that true?" he said, before repeating it to Mamta.

Tricia nodded, as she watched the embers of the fire glowing beneath the ashes.

SIX

AFTER a minute or two, Mamta began to speak. Her voice was low and she paused from time to time, letting Gautam translate. Tricia was hypnotized by the sound of her story as much as by the words. Gautam too spoke softly, but inside the hut even the slightest whisper was audible.

"I have grown quite ugly now but I was beautiful when I was a girl and when I used to go out into the forest to gather leaves for my father's cattle, the boys would chase after me. They would tempt me with gifts but I was never interested and I could always run faster than them and knew the places where I could hide. They used to tease me and call me names. When I think of those boys, it makes me laugh. How silly I was to chase them off. I knew what they were hoping for but I thought that I would save myself for someone else. It seemed so stupid now, to think of how I ran away from those boys, when I was still so young.

"One day my mother told me that they had arranged my marriage to a man from one of the villages nearby where my relatives lived. I had never met him before and I was innocent. Obviously he had some money, some land and a few cattle. He was also willing to take me cheaply. I agreed, for I had been expecting this for some time and I had prepared myself for marriage. There was a feast at my uncle's house and the groom's party came and all of the men got drunk, so drunk that there was no ceremony. They fell down around the fire and slept while my mother and some of the other women sat with me inside the hut.

"In the morning, my husband wakened from his stupor and came to get me. He was almost the same age as my father and when I first saw him, I hated him at once. His clothes were filthy from lying in the ashes near the fire and he had a grey, untidy beard and one of his ears was missing, cut away completely. He did not speak to me. My father was awake and he had begun to drink again along with the other men, so there was nobody to walk with me to the edge of the village. I went with him, carrying the small trunk which my mother and I had packed. I was crying so hard that when I looked back to see my home for the last time it was nothing but a blurr. We walked

148

all morning and the handle of the trunk dug into my fingers until I finally put it on my head and carried it that way. My husband did not speak at all.

"Along the way, we stopped at the home of someone my husband knew and they gave him some drink and they gave me some tea and some bread to eat. He got drunk again, and as we carried on towards his village, we were passing through a jungle. He suddenly turned on me and tried to take me right there on the path, grabbing at my clothes. The trunk fell from my head and hit him on the back. I did it by accident and he was not hurt that badly but he got angry with me and began to hit me across the face. For a few minutes, I did nothing, only tried to shield myself with my hands but he was in a frenzy and kept beating me until I thought that if I didn't run away, he would surely kill me. It was not too difficult to free myself, since he'd been drinking and I was able to escape, running through the forest away from the path. He chased me for a way but I was too quick for him and after a short distance, he gave up. There was nothing for me to do but run. I was frightened, terrified that he would beat me again. But where could I go? My parents would never take me back, not after they had given him my dowry. And even if I did go back to them, he would return and find me.

"It was getting dark and I had never been in this part of the forest before. I was not frightened, not of animals or spirits. They seemed so much more gentle than my own people. That night I found a place to sleep in the shelter of an amla tree. I had no water but I picked some of the amla fruit and chewed it down to quench my thirst. There was blood on my face from where he'd hit me. I cannot call him my husband. He was a demon, with one ear torn off and only six teeth left in his mouth. I made a bed out of leaves and that night I heard a leopard calling, but I wasn't afraid. I wanted the leopard to come and eat me, so that nobody would ever find me or know what happened.

"In the morning I was awake at dawn and following a game trail through the jungle, I came to a water-hole where I washed my face. There was some swelling but I hardly felt the pain. I sat for a long time by the water hole, wondering what I should do. I sat so still and without a sound that two different herds of deer came to the water and drank and went away without even knowing that I was there. Finally, I ate some more of the amla fruit which I had gathered under the tree and set off again along the game trail. After a way, it came to a forest road which I followed, though whenever I saw a turning, I would go into the bushes because I was afraid of meeting someone. The road was deserted even though I could see the tracks of bicycles and jeeps in the dirt.

"Finally, I came to a railway crossing and I could see that the forest road led on to a small ring of huts and a building with a water tower. I decided to follow the railway tracks. By this time, I was very hungry and the fruit which I had picked was making me sick so that I couldn't eat it any more. I heard the sound of a train coming and thought that I would lie down across the rails and let the train crush me and tear me into little pieces. I thought of those hundreds of wheels cutting through my body and for a few seconds I decided to take my life. But when I actually saw the train roaring down upon me, I was too afraid. Instead, I hid in the bushes beside the embankment and watched the engine race past in a streak of steel and smoke and the carriages with their windows flashing by, the faces of the travellers looking out at me. I had no idea where the train was going but somehow I wanted to climb onto the train and ride away as far as I could go. When it was gone, I came out of my hiding place and followed the railway tracks again, stepping from one wooden sleeper to the next.

"After several hours, I saw that I was coming to a station. At first, I was afraid to show myself. I was still wearing my bridal clothes. I had some jewelry which I took off and hid in the corner of my scarf. The station was far away from my parents' village and I didn't think that anyone would recognize me there. Trying not to show that I was frightened, I walked up to the platform. My mother had given me a few coins and taking these I went to one of the vendors and bought something to eat. There were quite a few people on the platform, waiting for a train and I sat down next to a group of villagers, so that nobody would think I was alone. Most people just ignored me. A train came in a few minutes later, but it was going in the direction from which I'd come. By then it had grown dark. I found some newspapers and made a place to sleep because I was exhausted. That night I kept waking up to the sounds of the trains arriving and departing. I had never ridden one before and I was frightened. There was something about the station which made me feel so lonely, the people coming and going, the smell of coal smoke, the whistles of the trains, the blue lights of the engines and the red and green lanterns in the switchyards. I had nobody in the world who cared for me. I could not go back home for they would send me to my husband's village. And he would certainly beat me. Everyone on the platform seemed to be going somewhere. They had their destinations, their journeys, their families. I was totally alone and as I lay there on the platform that night, it seemed as though I would always be this way and would go on walking forever, from station to station until finally I had the courage to throw myself onto the rails and die.

"When I awakened there was bright sunlight in my eyes. I could hear a child crying and the sound seemed to come from inside of me. I saw a woman holding a baby and with her there were two more children. She was trying to calm the child. I lay there and pretended to be sleeping. They were not far away, a few feet, no more. The baby had been startled by a train which had just pulled in and after a few minutes it fell asleep. I lifted myself up and watched the woman as she covered the baby with a cloth. She looked around and saw me watching her. I smiled at her and she seemed quite friendly. The other two children were pulling at her arms. I think they were hungry and she seemed confused and didn't want to leave the baby. Finally, she asked me if I was staying there for a while and would I sit beside the baby while she took the other two children with her. I said that I would and moved across and sat beside their luggage. The woman thanked me and went outside the station to a tea shop nearby.

"I sat there and watched the baby sleeping. She was so small and helpless. Her hands were tiny and as she slept, she opened and closed her fingers. After a few minutes the whistle on the train blew loudly and she woke up startled, opening her eyes and reaching out with her arms. I knelt and picked her up. She didn't seem to weigh anything at all. I thought that she would cry, but she only stared at me with those large black eyes. I was a stranger but she was not frightened and for the first time since I had left my home, I did not feel lonely or afraid. The little girl was wearing only a shirt and she was wrapped in a cotton shawl. I wished that I could have my own child, my own little girl like her to hold forever. I did not want to give her back to the woman.

"Just then the whistle blew again and the train began to move, the carriages sliding past me slowly. I don't know what it was that made me do it but suddenly I stood up, still holding the girl in my arms and ran across the platform to the nearest carriage. I almost missed my footing on the step but grabbed the handle and pulled myself inside the door. The carriage was not full and I made my way inside, seeing the station pass out of sight beyond the windows. The baby began to cry a little but I comforted her and found a seat. The others in the train were watching me but no one seemed suspicious or alarmed. I kept listening for the shouts and cries but nobody raised a sound and soon the train was travelling faster and faster through the countryside.

"It was the first time that I had been on a train and I could not believe how fast it went. I held the baby tightly as though she was the most precious thing in the world. Nothing mattered any more, for I was not alone. The baby was mine and I did not feel guilty about her mother. Let her weep, I thought. She has two of her own already. You cannot understand how much I loved this baby. I had held her in my arms for only a few minutes but she was mine and I would never let her go."

When Mamta stopped talking the only sound was the stirring of a goat in the hay at one corner of the hut. The fire died down completely and there was hardly any light.

"So, this is the truth," said Mamta. "This is how I stole you from your mother. I don't know who she was. The two of us had spoken maybe eight or ten words at the most. I don't know where she came from and honestly I don't even remember the station's name. If there was anything more which I could tell you, I would say it now. You might hate me for what I have done, hate me for taking you away that morning, but honestly I could not help myself. It was an impulse, an instinct which made me pick you up and run to the open doorway of that carriage. If I had fallen, we might have both been crushed beneath the wheels."

"How did you come to Pipra?" said Tricia.

"As we were riding on the train, the conductor came by and I realized that I had no ticket. I bribed him with the few coins which I had left and at the next station, I got down. It was a much larger place and I decided to go into the town and sell my jewelry so that I would have some money. I was worried that somebody would catch me and the police would hear about the stolen baby and they would take you from me.

"I found a goldsmith and sold my earrings for thirty rupees. I know that they were worth much more but I needed to buy you milk. Up until then I hadn't thought of how I would feed you and when I got the money, I went to a tea shop and had them warm some milk. You drank a little, though I think that you were not used to drinking from a cup and most of it spilled out the corners of your mouth. I bought some fruit and you ate part of a banana which I mashed between my fingers. I had no idea how to take care of a child and I spent some of the money on a toy, a rattle which was too big for you to hold. I was so foolish and did not know how to save my money. I bought some clothes for you. Then I got onto a bus. I was afraid of going to the station again because they might have heard about the stolen baby. We rode the bus to some other town. I think it was Madinpur, where I sold some more of my jewelry. By then I had made up the story about my husband being dead and I had told it to several people. They seemed to believe what I was saying and felt sorry for me.

"In Madinpur, I stayed in a dharamshala at the temple where one of the women from the bus had taken me. They let me sleep there for several days but then they made some excuse to put me out. You were not eating very much and when you cried, I felt so desperate and afraid. You didn't like the milk I bought for you and I spent all my money buying things to eat, biscuits and fruit. After a few days you got very sick, vomiting everything you ate or drank and such a fever too, as if you were going to burn up in my hands. I had no money left and I went to a chemist shop in Madinpur. The chemist gave me some syrup, even though I could not pay him. He was the one who told me about the hospital in Pipra and said that I should take you there. I had no money for a ticket and so I decided to walk. I followed the railway tracks just as I had done before I found you. Along the way, I asked whomever I met and that was how I got to Pipra."

Mamta turned her face aside for a moment and the dim glow from the fire outlined her features in the darkness.

"You must not be angry with me," said Mamta, "I was only a girl."

"I am not angry," said Tricia.

"But I have destroyed everything for you," said Mamta. "How can you forgive me?"

"There's nothing to forgive," said Tricia, touching Mamta on the arm. "I will always think of you as my mother."

After he had finished repeating what she'd said, Gautam lit a cigarette and the sudden brilliance of the match illuminated their faces. In that brief moment of light Mamta looked at both of them with love and sadness.

SEVEN

GHULAM RUSOOL was the only person at home when Tricia returned. He was cooking lunch and the smell of frying onions permeated the bungalow. After getting Tricia a glass of water from the ancient kerosene refrigerator, the old cook watched her drink with an inquisitive smile on his face.

"More?" he asked, when she had finished.

"No thank you," she said.

"Night-time sleeping?" he asked.

"Oh, I spent the night in the jungle," she said. "Kaproli."

Ghulam Rusool shook his head and frowned with disapproval.

"Tiger," he said, with a fierce grimace of his toothless mouth.

"Really?" said Tricia, laughing at his concern. "I didn't see any."

He stared at her with his rheumy eyes for a moment and Tricia thought of saying something about Mamta, but stopped herself. The old cook turned back to the stove.

"Ghulam Rusool," said Tricia. "Where is Dr Fry?"

"Hospital," he said, stirring the onions on the fire.

Gautam and Tricia had walked all the way back from Kaproli instead of catching the bus. Once they were in sight of the compound, however, Gautam said he had some work to do in Pipra. He pointed out the path that Tricia should follow and then headed off towards town with a hurried wave of his hand. Though he had made some excuse about visiting the Government Health Officer, Tricia could tell that Gautam didn't want to be seen arriving back with her. She didn't really mind and understood that he was probably doing it more for her sake than his own. Tricia knew that there was sure to be a flurry of compound gossip about her spending the night alone with Gautam in the forest. It was almost funny to think about the sort of things that they would say.

After bathing out of the tin bucket, Tricia went across to the hospital. She wanted Fry to know that she was back, but at the same time she wasn't sure what she would say to him. There was that uncomfortable feeling of knowing a secret and wishing now that she could forget what she'd been told.

At the gate of the hospital Tricia saw a group of people walking together, carrying something on their shoulders. As they turned onto the road, she saw that it was a dead body tied to a bamboo litter and wrapped in white cloth. She could see the shape of the body under the cloth but the face was covered. It seemed so thin and small. There were only men in the crowd and they looked solemn, though none of them were crying. Tricia waited for the procession of mourners to pass. One or two of them glanced at her with uncertain eyes. Tricia guessed that they were taking the body to the cremation ground. Once the group had gone a little way down the road, she started towards the entrance of the hospital.

Just then, Tricia saw the iron lung. It was lying on its side under one of the neem trees. Tricia turned and slowly walked towards it. The hatch was open and one of the bamboo struts had snapped. Tricia kneeled down cautiously and touched the handlebars. She ran her fingers along the seat. The machine seemed so crude and useless, like a piece of junk. She turned the pedals slowly with her hand and listened to the soft, mechanical breathing of the pump. Suddenly she felt a sense of panic and ran towards the hospital.

As she went in, the smell of formaldehyde was sharp enough to bring tears to her eyes. Pushing her way through the door of the general ward, Tricia looked into the expectant faces of more than a dozen women who turned to stare at her. Tricia's eyes moved to the last bed at the end of the ward. There were no nurses around but a man was standing with his back to her, looking down at the bed. Tricia hurried past the other patients until she came to the foot of the bed.

The man was Padre Massey, Gautam's father. He had his head bowed and one hand was resting on the girl's forehead. She was awake and looked at Tricia with a fixed expression in her eyes, a disquieting innocence. The tube had been removed from her throat and in its place there was a white gauze bandage. Tricia waited silently while Padre Massey finished his prayer. His lips were moving but there was no sound. His eyes were closed. He was wearing a white shirt, with the sleeves buttoned at the wrists and a necktie with yellow chevrons in a pattern down the front. His trousers were loose but belted tightly at the waist. He seemed quite different from the times she'd seen him before, in the pulpit of the church and at the graveside. Without his cassock he seemed less distant and affected. After a whispered amen, he turned and looked at Tricia. As if by reflex, he put his hand on her head and smiled.

"Hello," said Tricia, self consciously. "How is she doing?"

"Better," he said, looking down at the girl. "She is breathing more easily now. But there is still no movement in her legs."

"You were praying for her," said Tricia.

"Yes," he said. "Like the doctors, I also do my rounds."

"What did you pray for?" she asked.

He seemed puzzled by the question. His English was formal and correct but he spoke with hesitation.

"For her recovery," said Padre Massey. "So that she might walk again and play as other children."

"Is she a Christian?" asked Tricia.

He shook his head.

"You think that God will heal her?" said Tricia.

"Of course," said Padre Massey. "If that is his intention."

The girl was watching them, but Tricia could tell that she understood nothing of what they said. There was a stillness about her, the thin shape of her body beneath the white bedsheet. Only her eyes moved.

"I've met your son, Gautam," said Tricia. "He's been very helpful."

"My prodigal son," said Padre Massey. "He does not speak to us any more."

Tricia could see the pain in his eyes, even though he said it almost lightly.

"Do you still love him?" said Tricia.

"I am his father," said Padre Massey.

"But you're ashamed of him?" said Tricia.

"No. Why should I be ashamed?" said Padre Massey, "I only wonder why he stays in Pipra. He should get away. Here he only grows to hate us all the more."

"Yesterday, he took me to see Mamta," said Tricia.

Padre Massey didn't seem to understand, as though distracted by his thoughts.

"My mother," said Tricia.

He paused for a moment and finally nodded.

"I had forgotten," said Padre Massey. "Where is she now?"

"She lives in the forest, near Kaproli."

Tricia watched for his reaction, but Padre Massey seemed uninterested. He did not ask her any more and turned to look at the other women in the ward. There was an awkward silence. The girl was still staring at them with her dark and watchful eyes.

"Were you looking for Dr Fry?" he asked.

"Yes, I guess I was."

"He's in the workshop, at the back," said Padre Massey.

"All right. I'll find him. Thank you" she said.

"Goodbye," said Padre Massey and once again he touched her head lightly with his hand, a gesture of blessing and farewell.

Tricia went down the hall past the courtyard, which was used for the out-patients' clinic. There was a long verandah opening off the private wards. At the end of the verandah was a screened doorway which led to the enclosed area at the back of the hospital, where the kitchens and the workshop had been built. Tricia could hear the sound of an electric saw and as she came around one corner of the workshop, there was Dr Fry wearing his khaki shorts as usual, stooped over a low workbench and cutting a long board into narrow strips. The noise from the saw was almost unbearable, the shriek of wood and metal. Sawdust was flying everywhere and Fry had on a pair of dark glasses to protect his eyes. His entire concentration was directed to the board which he was cutting and he did not notice Tricia. There were a number of others watching also. Tricia had no idea what he was making but there was something very dignified about him, even as he worked, a simple man who enjoyed using his own two hands. He looked so unlike a surgeon, except for the care with which he measured the board before he cut another strip, using a straight edge and a pencil which he tucked behind one ear. Tricia watched, not wanting to disturb him at his work.

Part Five
DEPARTURE

AT THE STATION, there was the usual rush of people getting on the train, a clamour of voices and the shrill songs of a play-back singer on the radio. My compartment was crowded with villagers and luggage. I was fortunate to get a seat beside the window. The days were cooler now but the carriage had been standing in the sun and only one of the fans was working. Two railwaymen went past carrying green flags and a long-handled hammer. The train was only meant to stop in Pipra for a few minutes but it had already been there for a quarter of an hour. It was running late as usual. The assistant station master stood near the door of his office, watching the confusion with a dissolute scowl. He wore a white uniform which bagged at the knees and his brass buttons were badly tarnished, but he gave the appearance of superiority while those around him fled like birds in a storm from one end of the platform to the other.

There was a man selling peanuts and I beckoned to him, realizing that I hadn't eaten since the night before. He gave me a rupee's worth in a paper bag which had been made out of an old examination paper. As I ate the peanuts, I read the questions. They seemed to be the same as those I answered when I was in high school, chemistry questions about filtration rates and compound formulae. The peanuts were raw and full of sand. A magazine seller went by, screaming obscenities and for the first time I noticed that under the grime and soot of the station's ceiling there was a wrought-iron motif around the tops of the pillars holding up the beams. It was a stylized, floral design and might have been quite beautiful if someone had cleaned it up and scraped away the layers of paint. I wondered who it was that thought to put it there under the roof of this nondescript station, the last place in the world that anyone would expect a whimsical touch of decoration.

The train's whistle was like the cry of a lost animal. For a moment, the crowds on the platform grew even more frenzied and chaotic until the carriages creaked and jostled forwards against their couplings. I watched the faces dissolve, heard the last shouts of farewell. A child was waving but not to me. Slowly the engine gathered speed and the carriages broke away from the station, into the sunlight, the shadows peeling away from the windows. I caught a glimpse of a yellow sign with black lettering – PIPRA. Sitting back in my seat, I lit a cigarette as though it were a slow fuse and closed my eyes.

They will wonder where I have gone. The only person whom I told was Mamta and she would not believe me when I said that I was leaving. My parents, of course, will be relieved. Our quarrels seem so petty now. It was foolish of me to have rebelled in the way that I did, flaunting my name, my politics, my disbelief. I do not hate my mother any more. Her knees have almost crippled her and she can hardly walk. My father has become more distant with each year. I hadn't even noticed that he was growing old. They will never understand what I have done. The compound gives them a feeling of security and my parents will live the rest of their lives in Pipra. The church is their identity, their pride, their universe and I am sure that some day my mother and father will both go to heaven and it will be like a giant mission compound with celestial bungalows and angels watering the gardens of white flowers. Ruth will be there to greet them and Miss Reynolds too, wearing her nurse's uniform. It will be like old times again. But I will be somewhere else, not hell exactly, not the fiery inferno of the brick kiln, but a kind of fair ground full of all the hideous grotesques of nature, the godchild in its bottle, Mr Samson and the mating dogs . . .

The train crosses over the canal bridge and I feel as though I have passed through a barrier, moving beyond the boundaries of my childhood, out into the unknown world.

Dr Fry will be surprised that I have left, but I know that he will understand. He seemed much happier after Patricia's visit, less isolated in his work. Patricia left just over a week ago, travelling by the same train that I am riding, the same train that Miss Reynolds took her on, almost twenty years ago. She said that she might come back some day, but I could tell that we would never see each other again. We did not get a chance to say goodbye because I got delayed while I was up in the hills, visiting two of our villages. Perhaps it was better that way. I returned the morning after she had gone. There was a note from her which said that she was sorry to leave without seeing me. She also thanked me for whatever I had done.

I have always enjoyed train journeys. The landscape races past and I can only see the countryside in glimpses, a flash of colour, a smear of green and the constant blur of grey earth. It hardly matters where I am going. My ticket is as far as Jhansi where I will get down and wait all night for another train which will take me further east. I am still not sure if I will go as far as Bihar. My friend is not expecting me and it might just happen that I will find a station along the way which catches my interest, a small, forgotten town not unlike Pipra where I might find some work.

I have never felt this sort of freedom before, a sense of complete detachment. I can go anywhere in India. My needs are minimal. I am carrying nothing but a duffel bag. I have been released from all my memories.

That night, after she had told us what had happened, Mamta spread some straw on the ground and laid a quilt over the top. It made a comfortable bed. There was not enough room for all three of us on the cot and there was only one quilt. We slept together, Mamta in the middle and Patricia and I on either side. The smoke from the fire kept the mosquitoes away and I slept soundly until dawn when I found that Mamta had got up. Patricia was still asleep and I rose slowly so as not to wake her. When I went outside, I could see Mamta coming back from the stream, carrying a water vessel on her head. There was a pale, blue light and the sun was not yet up. From a distance she looked exactly the same as I remembered her, a girl of sixteen. She walked towards me and I thought how gracefully she moved, like a figure from a dream.